DREAMS IN FLAMES

A.W. SANDY

Dedication

To S.S., J.S., L.S., T.G., & A.W., you are all blessings. I love you all forever.

A.W. Sandy

Table of Contents

Salvo airlines flight 965- 2

Nina & Dominic- 18

The Island-34

Wedding bells-47

Connections-68

Dashed dreams-79

Dreams In Flames

"Ma'am, please take your seat. Do you know where to go?" A kind flight attendant inquired as she peered at Nina Saini, her glasses nearly falling off her face. Nina glanced around the massive interior of the plane, feeling her heart pound in her chest.

"Yeah, um…" she paused, glancing at some documents in her petite hands.

"Oh, yeah, um… it says SA-119, whereabouts is that?" Flashing a warm smile, the flight attendant gestured towards the back of the plane. "Let's get seated as soon as possible, honey. We're about to take off soon." Shuffling nervously and muttering a quick thank you, Nina sauntered to her seat and placed her duffle bag in the overhead storage. The window seat was occupied, and in it sat a handsome, exotic-looking man with long, shiny hair touching his shoulders. He looked up at her with dazzling hazel eyes and flashed a tantalizing smile. It was almost enough for the reserved photographer to melt right there. Shyly, she sat beside the gorgeous stranger, clearing her throat as she gestured towards the window.

"I don't know how people choose the window seat. It's so nerve-wracking!" The man pushed his headphones off his ears as he eyed the curly-headed woman with bright brown eyes. Nina's eyelashes fluttered incessantly as she adjusted herself on the leather airplane seat.

"Oh, the window seat? Hey now, it's the best seat you can get! You fly often?" The man asked curiously, smoothing his hair back. It was obvious he took amazing care of himself. Nina bit her lip, holding onto the arms of the chair.

"To be honest, rarely at all. I'm a photographer by trade; weddings, birthdays, bar mitzvahs, you name it. I'm from Chicago, and I usually stay local for work. This time, a client asked if I could travel to Turks and Caicos for their wedding… and let's just say, it was hard to refuse. But believe me, I'm very uncomfortable right now. I haven't flown in two decades." Nina's hands began tremoring on the arm stands. The man eyed her closely, noting her anxious state. He cleared his throat nervously. "Two decades! That's a really long time." He paused, glancing at Nina's beautifully manicured fingernails. "I'm Dominic McLeod. You are?"

Nina graciously met his hand, shaking it delicately as she gawked at him. He seemed to get more handsome as she stared at him. "Nina. Nina Saini."

Dominic glanced at Nina's hand and then slyly lifted it to his lips, planting a delicate kiss on it. Nina sank into her seat as Dominic watched her squirm, seemingly enjoying her reaction.

"Well, you've got nothing to worry about; it's a good thing they put you right beside me, huh?" He patted her knee and lightly squeezed. Nina was taken aback by the man's hands-on approach. She spoke up.

"Do you greet all the women you meet in the same way?" He cocked his eye at her once again, tossing his luscious hair back. It cascaded against the back of his seat. "I can tell you with full honesty that I've never met a woman as beautiful as you, so to answer your question, no, I don't do this often." She felt herself blushing as Dominic looked her over, glancing at her turquoise V-neck. His eyes traveled to her khaki shorts, and then to her roman inspired sandals. Her recently pedicured toes matched her shirt.

"You are really beautiful, I mean… wow! You've honestly made my day. My apologies if I'm coming on too strong, but wow, I really can't help it."

Nina giggled, loosening her grip slightly on the armrest. "Well, thank you. I just hope everything goes well. I'm so nervous!" Suddenly, there was a loud crashing that came from the front of the plane.

"Hey, watch it, that's hot! What, are you trying to burn me?" The pair looked at each other, a bit shaken, as they cocked their heads over their seats to watch the commotion. A heavy-set man waddled to the center of the plane, wiping something off his pant leg. "I paid a lot for this seat; I expect a different type of treatment!" He berated a flight attendant, who appeared to have spilled beverages off her tray. She hastily cleaned up the mess, apologizing profusely.

"My mistake, Sir. Please forgive me, this is my first week on the job." The man rolled his eye, snatching a drink off of another staff's tray. They glared at the man, bewildered. "Sir, we are very sorry for the spill, but we cannot have you taking someone else's order. Please get back into your seat, and once we are in the air, we'll make another drink for you, on the house!"

The man, unforgiving, gulped the drink in one go and tossed the glass to the floor of the plane. It shattered into multiple pieces, causing shrieks of concern from the traveling passengers.

"Okay, Sir, I'm sorry, we're going to have to remove you from the flight. Please retrieve your belongings from the storage, and security personnel will escort you." The obese man, fuming, aggressively glared around the airplane, sizing up the crowd.

"No one's speaking up for me, huh? So what's up with that? You all get to go on vacation to Turks and Caicos, and I get kicked off because these lousy people spilled my drink? Who wouldn't be mad?"

Nina looked over at Dominic, who nervously shrugged and mocked the man quietly, doing hand gestures. Nina giggled and lightly nudged him, signaling him to stop.

"Sir, the security is on the way, alright? You need to get off the plane immediately. Grab your items, and let's go." The man sneered, clearly incensed, but complied and retrieved a small suitcase from the overhead storage. He waved a fist around, still eyeing the sea of holiday goers. "You all make me sick. Live it up in Caicos, bitches!" Shocked murmurs rang through the plane just as security entered and put handcuffs around the man; his suitcase tumbling to the ground. It hit the corner of a seat and the latch popped off, sending the contents flying down the aisle. Among the items were a can of shaving cream and an adult sex toy. Giggles and spats of laughter echoed through the interior of the massive jet as security scrambled to pick up the items and place them back into the now compromised suitcase. The man turned red as a beet.

"You all owe me a drink and a new suitcase! You'll be hearing from my lawyer!" The crowd cheered as they led the man off the plane, expletives rolling off his tongue. Dominic tapped the window with his finger, unable to hold his laughter back.

"Wow! That was better than any movie that they play on these damn planes! They should have kept him on." Nina rolled her eyes, watching through the grounded plane window. "No! He was violent, it's good they took him off. Funny antics, sure, but a tad scary. He was drunk, or maybe on drugs. Probably both." Dominic cocked his head back with laughter, tapping Nina's knee. She recoiled, glancing at him, bewildered.

"You're very hands-on, aren't you?"

"I mean… is it bothering you?"

"Well, I am a stranger, right? Do you touch every stranger you see?"

"Hey, you were the one who was hyperventilating from fear of being on the plane, right? I'm just trying to calm you done." Nina dropped her head, biting her lip. Dominic, realizing he struck a chord, cleared his throat, attempting to reconcile.

"Hey, listen. I am so sorry; that was really insensitive of me." Nina's eyes watered as an announcement echoed through the plane.

"Good afternoon, ladies and gentlemen, this is your pilot, Silas Davies. Joining me on this flight is Co-Pilot Viviane Boyd, and we want to start by thanking you for choosing Salvo Airlines. It's an absolute pleasure to be a part of the flight team, and we've got some brief information to share with all of you." Dominic softly nudged Nina, who briskly wiped away tears from her face. "Hey, listen… I am so sorry; I didn't mean what I said." Nina blinked through tears, taking in a deep breath.

"No, you're right. You're absolutely right. I'm such a wuss. I just need to trek through this. To be honest, I should have taken my mother's advice and gotten my doctor to prescribe me some sleeping pills. Thing is, I hardly take any form of medication, so I was leery about it." Dominic nodded quietly, squeezing her knee. "Well, I still shouldn't have said anything, and I apologize. Here I am, sitting beside the most beautiful woman I've ever seen, and I make her cry. I'm such a fuckup." Nina giggled, wiping her clammy palms on her shorts. "Don't sweat it, honest! It's okay."

Over the speakers, the pilot continued.

"We're en route to the beautiful Caribbean island of Turks and Caicos, and we are expecting a pleasant, smooth ride. The current time is 1:15 PM, and this flight will take about six hours, with an approximate arrival time of 7:15 PM. The forecast is calling for overcast skies with the chance of light rain. If you require any support or assistance, we've got an excellent team of stewards and stewardesses at the ready. We all wish for you to have a restful, enjoyable flight."

Nina inhaled deeply, feeling her stomach flutter with anxiety. She looked over to Dominic, who was hopelessly gazing out the window.

Tapping him lightly on the shoulder, he looked at her with melancholy eyes. "I'm sorry, I feel so crappy now!" Nina leaned into him, her lips making light contact with his ear. "Can I hold your hand? I'm terrified." Dominic's eyes widened, but he happily obliged, clasping Nina's hand as though his life depended on it. At that moment, a tall, slender woman with bright ginger hair stood at the front of the plane, her bright green eyes twinkling under the powerful cabin lights.

"Hello, I am stewardess Nestani, and I will be going over some emergency safety procedures before we take off. I encourage everyone, if possible, to take notice of these procedures, as it helps us all be safe and aware of our responsibilities aboard our flight."

Nina sucked in a breath, squeezing Dominic's hand.

"This is what I was dreading."

Dominic patted her hand, then ran his fingers over it, taking notice of how soft she was.

"This is just protocol, Nina. Nothing to worry about. I'm here for you, remember? I won't leave you alone." Gulping but nodding in agreement, she cocked her head nervously toward the flight attendant, who was using grand expressions with her body. She appeared like she was on Broadway.

"In the case of an emergency that requires evacuation, we must be able to get on our life jackets if we plan on doing an emergency landing in water. This is vital to sustaining lives and remaining safe. These life jackets are located in the compartment under your seats. In the event that life jackets are needed, you take them from the compartment and place them over your head. After doing so, clip the waistband on, and pull tightly, to ensure it is snug and fits you well." Passengers nodded and murmured amongst themselves, paying close attention to the flight attendant as she demonstrated the procedure in front of them. Nina groaned, feeling her stomach perform somersaults. The stewardess continued.

"Do not inflate the life jackets until we have ushered you out of the aircraft. There are designated doors that are used in the case of an evacuation. Our crew would assist everyone, to ensure you all exit the aircraft promptly but safely. Concerning oxygen masks, these will be dropped in front of you if an emergency presents itself. If this happens, please pull the mask towards your face and affix it to your mouth and nose. If any of you are traveling with children, ensure you are breathing through the mask first, and then your child. With the mask on your face, breathe normally."

Dominic leaned into Nina. His breath felt hot on her neck, and she felt herself blushing. "It's all pretty mundane. All of this, really, but they've got to do it. Think about it: when we land in Turks and Caicos, you're going to forget all your worries. Which resort are you staying at?" Nina turned to face him, not sure if she should give her information but doing so anyway. "I'm booked at Ivory Shores Resort." Dominic nodded, remaining in close proximity to her face. He felt himself glancing at her plump lips, feeling the urge to kiss them tenderly. The feelings overtaking him were foreign, and he was trying his best to combat them. He felt like a creep.

Nina felt the heat rising between them, and the words of the stewardess got drowned out. She looked Dominic over, feeling herself get faint as she continued to hold on to his hand. Nina wasn't the type of person to date. She hardly went out unless it had to do with work. But she couldn't help but feel like she knew Dominic. They had just met; she knew this, but the way he was making her feel was becoming all too overwhelming. Dominic looked down, gnawing back at the intense emotions that were overpowering him. He was a single man on vacation. No kids, no wife. He couldn't comprehend how he got so lucky; to be sitting beside such a beautiful, albeit petrified, woman. He was a man who was used to standing up for what was right, and at that moment, he knew only to do one thing. Scanning Nina's face, he rubbed her thigh, and he looked at his hand as he did so, as though he could not believe what he was doing. Nina glanced around nervously; worried other passengers could see what was happening. Luckily, their attention was all focused on the animated stewardess.

"Dominic, what are you doing?" she whispered, watching his hand trail over her leg. Heat slithered up her neck, and she tried focusing on the window next to Dominic, noticing how the sun's rays danced over the tarmac. Dominic leaned into her lips, planting a wet kiss on her face. Nina instantly pulled away, ashamed that a stranger was showing such affection to her. Part of her felt it was wrong, but as she glanced at Dominic and saw the glazed look in his eyes, she could tell that he was gentle; he didn't mean any harm. Something greater than them was controlling the momentum between them, and it was as though they could not do anything to combat the mounting sexual tension.

Returning the favor, Nina kissed Dominic's lips timidly. His stomach fluttered.

"You're so beautiful." He swooped in for a kiss, but a terrified Nina pulled back, appalled. "Dominic, stop! We don't know each other! You and I are strangers to each other and just met! We know that this isn't okay; strangers don't go kissing each other." Dominic bit his lip, imagining what it would be like if she were in his bed.

"The strange thing is, Nina, I don't feel like we're strangers. If we are, we're definitely the *strange* type." Nina giggled, rolling her eyes at the ridiculously bad joke. "I'm serious! Come on, this is weird. Let's just stop and try to maintain some integrity here." Though as she said these words, she couldn't help but feel the warmth between her legs. Dominic was doing something to her. He spoke up, making sure the space between them stayed sealed.

"Listen, I'm staying at Onyx Renaissance Resort and Spa. Forget Ivory Shores; I want you to come with me. If they charge you any cancellation fees, I'll take care of them. I just… I just don't want to lose the opportunity to get to know you." Nina put her hand up in protest.

"Dominic, you know I couldn't let you do that. I paid a lot for my resort, almost three grand. I couldn't let you pay for that. Besides, you don't even know me! I just can't allow it." Swiftly, Dominic hushed her, placing his finger against her lips.

"I don't care about the cost. I don't mean to brag, but I'm an attorney, so… money isn't a problem for me. If you feel I'm coming off strong, well, so be it. I think I might hate myself if you walk away, and I never get to see you again."

Nina perked up. "You're an attorney? What's your specialty?" Dominic scoffed, remembering his most recent case with a family embroiled in a bitter divorce. "Family law. It'll definitely drain the life out of you if you let it. Luckily, I love what I do, and I get paid well for it. Please, Nina. Please! Come to my resort, let's spend some time together, and get to know each other. I promise all costs will be on me."

Nina looked away, just as a voice came over the speaker. The flight attendant was no longer standing in the aisle.

"Ladies and gentlemen, at this time, we ask you all to sit in your seats and fasten your seatbelts, as we are next in line for take-off. Ensure all table trays are in an upright position and all baggage is secured under your seats or in your overhead baggage compartment. All cell phones and other electronic devices must be switched off and, of course, smoking is completely prohibited for the duration of the flight. We all hope you enjoy your time on flight 965."

Nina squeezed Dominic's hand, using the other to ensure her seatbelt was firmly clasped shut.

"Okay, Dominic. I'll go with you. I'll go. Please, just hold on to me, and don't let go, okay?" Dominic's eyes danced excitedly as he looked on at his new female companion, eager to learn more about her.

At that moment, the plane taxied down the runway, and Nina felt every vibration ripple through her stomach as the massive jet violently shook. Dominic smiled sweetly at her and, reaching into his pant pocket, he pulled out a stick of gum, gesturing for Nina to open her mouth. "The pressure, you know?" He gestured to his ears. Nina laughed, quickly accepting the minty gum.

"Lawyers are always prepared, right?" He let out a hearty laugh just as the plane lifted off the ground. Nina shut her eyes tight as her stomach did somersaults. Aggressively chewing on the gum, she clenched onto Dominic's hand and slowly opened one eye, attempting to look out his window.

"No, no no! Not doing that. Nope, no way!"

"It's alright, Nina, I'm here. Once we're at cruising altitude, everything's going to be just fine. It feels weird as hell right now, but I promise we'll be fine soon." She nodded, though the pressure of the intense movement kept her head firmly against the seat headrest. As they continued to rise, Nina's mind drifted to her severe phobia; it was shocking that she hadn't blacked out yet. Nina hadn't always been so fear-stricken. According to her parents, in fact, she had always enjoyed flying overseas as a child.

Her parents, Arya and Rahul, were avid travelers that enjoyed getting on a plane at least three times every year. They had taken Nina on many excursions when she was a child, and she thoroughly enjoyed having the window seat, seeing the world below shrink and the skies expand. She'd laugh and point and be completely awestruck at being on a plane. In fact, her parents actively had to calm her down, as she'd squeal and scream with such delight, she'd get quite the reaction from other vacationers. There was one instance, however, that shook Nina to her core, and caused her to fall into a deep phobia that she wasn't able to get out of.

When Nina was thirteen, she and her parents decided to travel to London, England, for summer vacation. Her mom, being a registered nurse, and her father, a cardiologist, had always spoken about traveling there but had not come around to it, as they always ended up going to a tropical island instead.

On this flight, the turbulence was severe. The massive jet had shaken violently, throwing anyone and anything not strapped down across rows of chairs. Debris was airborne; hot beverages spilled on passengers, causing burns. Nina remembered clasping onto her armrests until her knuckles turned white. Her parents tried to reassure her that everything was going to be fine, but they too had looks of extreme fear etched on their faces.

Nina glanced out the window, but the shaking sensation distorted her vision. Across the aisle, a man projectile vomited all over another passenger, and at seeing that, Nina closed her eyes and heaved. Many children in the plane were wailing with fear, and their parents were attempting to soothe them, but it wasn't working. The noises emanating from the plane were outrageously loud, and the violent turbulence was sending her into an emotional tailspin. Nina remembered little after that because she passed out.

When she came to, she was in a hospital, and her parents sat at her bedside, eyes widened at the sight of her sitting up.

"Nina! My Nina, are you alright, dear?" Her mother wailed. Nina's eyes fluttered as she glanced her mother and father over. He kissed Nina on the forehead and held her tight, tears filling his eyes.

Being a doctor, Nina knew her father was used to seeing people from all walks of life in terrible conditions. She knew, at that moment, that her father was deeply affected by his own child in a hospital bed. "Where am I? What happened?" Nina asked warily, her head feeling cloudy.

"Dear, you passed out on the airplane after the turbulence we experienced. Everyone's okay and

you're okay. After you lost consciousness, the plane
had to turn around, and we rushed you here."

Nina, through her confusion and fear, felt bad for her
parents. They didn't get to go to London, and it was
because she couldn't get through some turbulence.
Remembering the jarring event, she made a promise
to herself. "I'll never fly again."

Shaking the memory out of her head, she looked at
Dominic, whose eyes were closed. He had a serene
look on his face, as though he were enjoying the
climb. Nina felt foolish. She had not been on a plane
for over twenty years, and the fear she felt as a
thirteen-year-old still made her blood run cold.
Overhead, the pilot spoke confidently, a sing-song
cadence apparent in his voice.

"Hello again, passengers of flight 965. It's Captain
Davies again. Currently, we are cruising at 31,000
feet. The skies are slightly overcast, but the view is
stunning." The vacationers chatted in agreement,
aweing at the spectacular views from their windows.

"At this time, the cabin crew will be making their
way around to you, taking orders for light
refreshments, if you so choose to have any. Movies
and shows are available to watch on your monitors,
so please enjoy. Before reaching our wonderful
destination, I will check in with all of you once more.
Once again, enjoy the flight." Dominic danced in his
seat as the cabin of the plane became louder and more
animated, with some folks standing up and stretching.
"Do you want a drink?" Dominic inquired, flipping
his hair out of his face. Nina placed her hand on her

chest, stunned that she got through the take-off so well. She glanced at Dominic, dumbfounded.

She told herself she'd never board a plane again, but here she was, panicked, but alive and well. Dominic had an effect on her, and she was willing to pay him back for keeping her calm and safe.

"I'll have a rum and coke. I can't believe I'm okay."

Nina & Dominic

After downing two rum and cokes with Dominic and watching a movie as he slept, Nina stayed on guard as she forced herself to not look out of the window. Sure, Dominic had done a phenomenal job of keeping her calm, but that didn't change the fact that she was miles up in the sky, with no chance of escape. Firmly in her seat, she turned her head ever so slightly, attempting to challenge herself to peer out of the window, but as soon as the corner of her eye met the circular window, she'd snap her head back and close her eyes shut, reciting prayers in her head.

She had to use the bathroom desperately but was so apprehensive about doing so, as she was afraid of what would happen if she stood up. With fear mounting her gut, she bit her lip and shook Dominic awake, adjusting her top as she did so.

He woke up with a jolt and wiped the corners of his mouth as he straightened himself in his seat. Dominic smiled at her, but he could see the concern on her face. "Nina, what's wrong?"

She looked down, ashamed.

"I have to go to the washroom, but… I'm scared." Dominic, without hesitation, unbuckled his seatbelt, which Nina followed promptly. She wasn't going anywhere with it firmly clasped around her lap, anyway. "Anything you need, just ask. You don't need to be bashful about it. Come, let me take you."

Gesturing for her to stand, she shakily rose to her feet, and, while keeping her head down, allowed Dominic to lead the way to the washroom. Since they were already at the back of the plane, they didn't have far to go, but Nina didn't care. She felt an extreme sensation of vertigo, and her knees felt like jelly. Dominic sensed this and graciously held onto her trim waist, guiding her to the lavatory.

"It's okay, I got you. It's alright, I'm here."

"Dominic, don't let me go, please."

"I'm here, don't worry."

They approached the washroom doors and Dom squeezed her hand tenderly. "Do you… do you want me to go in there with you?" Nina laughed nervously, but she was visibly shaking. "No, I think I'll be okay. Just please, stay outside of the door. I'll need your help to go back." Dominic put his hand over his chest, surrendering himself to her. "I'll be right here."

Nodding, Nina awkwardly shuffled into the tiny space, apprehensively shutting the door behind her. Dominic tossed his hair about as he struggled to keep himself composed. He was a man that was taught to compose himself in difficult situations; being a lawyer showed him in more ways than one. This situation was unlike any he had ever experienced. Here he was, an overworked, single lawyer heading off into glorious sun rays, and stunning beaches. Dominic felt like he hit the jackpot, and he wasn't about to share his winnings. He wanted Nina all to himself, and he was going to make sure nothing interfered with that. After a few minutes, the door opened and Nina reappeared, displaying a look of discomfort. "That was not fun, I'll tell you that." She quickly positioned herself beside Dominic, holding onto his arms for dear life. "You want to try to look out of a window?" Nina shook her head aggressively, snapping her eyes shut. "Please, Dominic. Not now. Let's just get back to our seats. I can't be up for a minute more." Patting her hand sympathetically, he led her back to their seats, and they sat, Dominic, laughing at the fact that Nina's eyes were still shut.

"You can open your eyes now, and you better anyway, because I think we're almost here."

Dominic peered out of the window, excitement running through his veins. The plane soared over the crystal-clear waters of Turks and Caicos. The water rippled and gleamed like diamonds; it was a fabulous sight to behold. Opening one eye slowly, Nina looked at the window and instantly felt her stomach churn. She wanted to enjoy the view, but her fear overtook her.

"Let's talk about something else." She gulped hard. Dominic smiled shrewdly. "Okay, why not! Why don't you tell me about what you do?"

"Can you cover the window first, though?" Without hesitation, Dominic did as she requested. Breathing a sigh of relief, she began to relax a little, though she still felt a bit queasy.

"Well, I'm a photographer. I was always interested in art, but I knew drawing wasn't my thing. After

exploring a few clubs in high school, I decided my
calling was photography, and I've been doing it ever
since! At first, I wasn't trying to make it a career; I
genuinely liked it because it was a hobby! Over time,
though, I was garnering a lot of attention for my
work, and my family encouraged me to make a
business of it!" Dominic sat forward, honing in on
every word. "Wow! That's inspiring. I like that."
Nina blushed, playing with her fingernails.

"Well, thanks! I love what I do. The bulk of my work
is weddings, so that's always exciting. Some of my
friends think that I'm too shy to be a photographer.
They think I need to put more life in me if I want to
get far. Then, coincidentally, a client called me and
asked if I'd do their wedding photos in Turks and
Caicos. Of course, I was petrified; I haven't been on a
plane in years! But here I am! The things I do for
money." Dominic let out a heap of laughter, causing
Nina to squirm as she stifled chuckles.

"First, those friends that think you're too shy, they
don't know what they're talking about. Sounds like a
bunch of jealous people who don't have the guts to do
what you do. They don't have their own business, so
they can't stand to see someone they know do well
for themselves. Trust me, I've dealt with it too, so I
know this all too well. Second, you should be proud
of yourself! I wouldn't even say you're just doing this
for just the money. I'd bet on it that you really want
to get over your phobia of flying! And you're doing
it! You're doing it right here, right now, and you
ought to be proud of yourself. No wonder why these
people are jealous. You're out here, fighting against

the fear, but in the same stretch, traveling and doing what you do best and love!"

Nina sat back, taking in Dominic's words. This man, who she just met, understood her more than her childhood friends did. The thought made her feel a bit gloomy. Despite her conflicted feelings, she squeezed Dominic's knee in appreciation of his sentiments. "You're right. You're absolutely right. I don't even know how I'm on this plane, but I am, and I'm braving it out! It's pretty surreal, because I told myself I'd never go on one again, but you know what, I'm beating it, and though it's an enormous challenge, I'm trying, and that's what matters." She took a big gulp as Dominic scanned Nina's face benevolently.

"But Dominic, what about you? How did you get into law? I've never known anyone personally in the industry; how do you like it?" Dominic raised his head thoughtfully, truly pondering the reasons.

"I've always loved advocating for people, especially those who I felt didn't have a voice. There are so many problems in this world. How good would it be that we all could have someone in our corner, at all times, fighting for us and helping us regain order in our lives? I used to think about that a lot as a teen. When I was in high school, my professors used to tell me I'd be great in theatre, believe it or not! I was confused, but I think they thought there was something theatrical and animated about me that would lead me to join that industry. Sorry, but Broadway and anything attached to that weren't in the plans. However, it helped me later, when I became a lawyer. At first, I wanted to do employment law, but I found it to be dull; kind of boring. Family law was different. I could help individuals having the worst time of their lives, and that resonated well with me. Whenever there were kids involved, it always made the situation muddier. The children were always in the middle. It was sort of unavoidable."

Nina nodded, quite engaged in the conversation.

"Yeah, I could imagine! Those moments must have been trying, I'm sure. Having to remain professional and courteous, but at the end of the day, you feel real human emotions! Which is understandable, of course. Sometimes, you have to take care of yourself, too. Props to you, for sure, because I wouldn't be able to be a lawyer. I don't think I'd be a good advocate for anyone."

Dominic raised his eyebrow and then flashed a cheeky grin. "You're a talented photographer, and you're giving people gifts they can keep for a lifetime. You may not see yourself as an advocate, but at least you can say you're on the positive side, helping individuals from all walks of life capture special moments in time, forever." Nina blushed, covering her eyes with her hand. She wasn't used to getting compliments, but then again, all of this was foreign to her. Traveling on a plane after her traumatic experience? She would have never imagined it. Dominic rubbed her thigh, feeling elated. "What, you're shy? Well, we can fix that. By the end of your trip, you'll feel like you knew me your whole life. It's crazy, but I already feel like that right now." At that moment, the Captain began talking through the speakers.

"Hello, passengers of flight 965, we hope you've thoroughly enjoyed flying with Salvo Airlines. We are getting ready to land at Taboola International Airport, so we ask that you all fasten your seatbelts, and stay in your seats at this time. Any luggage or other belongings must be stowed away in the overhead storage or under your seats. We will be landing shortly. Thank you."

Without hesitation, Nina fastened her seatbelt, with Dominic swiftly following. "Here we go again! Please hold me." She offered her hand to Dominic, who promptly clutched her for support.

"Don't worry, I'm here." The plane began its descent over the clear waters, and Dominic was in awe at the spectacular view, having lifted the screen covering the window. The sky had darkened considerably, but it only made the island look more mystical. "I don't know why I'm only just coming to this island. I mean, I've been to a few. Grenada, St. Lucia, Jamaica, even. This, though, is different. The waters couldn't be more dazzling."

Nina grunted a response but kept her eyes firmly shut. She was content with getting the imagery from Dom's description. Nina couldn't bring herself to look out the window. She'd wait until she was safely on the ground to take in the sights. Ten minutes later, the plane made a safe touch down at Taboola Airport, and the vacationers cheered happily. Thunderous clapping rumbled on the immense jet.

Dominic danced in his seat as Nina opened her eyes. She burst out in laughter, giving his knee a playful tug. "I did it! This is unreal!" She squealed happily. Nina felt like she could cry, but somehow, she kept it together in the best way. Unhooking his seatbelt, he reached for Nina's and did the same for her. Nina bit her lip as Dominic's finger came into contact with her shirt, and he eyed her breasts, nearly licking his chops. "You know, just your friendly lawyer friend lending a helping hand."

Nina cocked her head back as the cabin of the plane stirred, with vacationers standing and retrieving their belongings. "Oh yeah, helping hand." She gestured air quotations. Dominic stood first, and helped Nina to her feet, sensing she'd be a bit unstable, and he was right. Nina seemed spatially disoriented as she rose and placed her palm on her head.

"It's been a long time, Dominic. I don't know. I think I have vertigo. It's something to do with the phobia, I'm sure." He smiled amiably.

"I've got you, so there's no need to worry."

Gathering their belongings and slowly inching their way out of the plane, Nina and Dominic made their way into Taboola Airport to start the journey to Onyx Resort.

"How were you going to get to the resort, Dominic? Call a cab, or…"

He winked as he led her to baggage claim, dodging the masses of people who were doing the same.

"Call a cab? No way, I have a car rental waiting, and you're hopping in with me. Let's get our stuff and head out. I'm excited to get some dinner, aren't you?"

Nina, taking in the surrounding sights, felt herself relax. She was off the plane, and that's all that mattered. Collecting their luggage and heading to the parking lot, Dominic found his rental and loaded their suitcases in the trunk. Sauntering to the passenger door, he kindly opened it for Nina, who hesitantly stepped inside. He spotted this and looked at her peculiarly. "What, you don't want to go in?"

Nina giggled softly, resting her hand on the top of the car. "It's not that, it's just… it almost doesn't feel real that I'm here! I mean, I know I am, but it's still unreal. It's so exciting, it's almost hard to believe." Dominic lifted Nina's hand and kissed it softly, donning a sly grin.

"Well, believe it! Photographer meets lawyer, who would have thought? Let's get this vacation started, shall we?" Nina rolled her eyes and crossed her arms over her breast, the corners of her mouth trembling as she stifled a smile. "Remember, I'm here on business!" Dominic cocked his head back in laughter.

"I don't think weddings are a week long. What day is the actual ceremony?"

"Saturday, so in two days."

"Oh, okay! So after that, your vacation technically begins! And since you don't have to work for two days, we'll start on the right foot, and get to know each other. Hey, if you want free legal advice, I'll give it to you, just in case you ever need it."

Unable to control herself, she flew into a fit of giggles as she inched herself into the passenger seat.

"Okay, okay! You've won me over!" She blurted out, covering her face to hide her reddened cheeks.

 Dominic closed the door behind her, flashing a proud grin.

"I think we won each other over the moment we both locked eyes on the plane." Nina sank into her seat as Dominic took his position in the driver's seat, and peeled out of the airport parking lot, heading to the main roads. As they traversed the streets, they took in beautiful sights of palm trees and rolling mountains that seemed to paint the sky. The sun's rays were astounding as they flickered on every surface, including the car they were traveling in.

"It's so beautiful, I can hardly believe it."

"Believe it, Nina! We're here. It's like we were both meant to cross paths. We both needed breaks from our busy lives and look where we're at now. It was meant to be. I just know it."

"I can't wait to call my parents and let them know I've arrived safely. They were always really worried about me, but I think it's partially my fault. I was always a timid, sensitive child, so they felt the need to always protect me from harm. I can't help but feel like I put a lot of pressure on them, especially because of my phobia. The anxiety got so bad that they sent me to therapists so that I could talk through my feelings. I felt so embarrassed after a while. When I told my parents I was going to Turks and Caicos for a client, they couldn't believe it. In fact, they thought I was making the wrong decision. Not because they didn't want me to make money or travel, it wasn't that. They saw how bad I used to get after the situation in my childhood. They knew I was easily triggered and still wounded from that experience. So, I think they thought my traveling would actually do more harm than good. I don't blame them, though."

Dominic tapped on the steering wheel as he listened to Nina intently, looking over at her angelic face every so often as her plump lips moved with every word spoken. "Don't take this the wrong way, but I feel like you're really hard on yourself, as though you believe you don't deserve happiness or good things, and you do! I'm sure your parents are lovely people who want the best for you. They probably never expected you to board a plane again, but that doesn't mean that deep down, they didn't wish for it. They wanted to protect you; keep you safe. You're their daughter, so it's natural. Call them as soon as we get to the resort. I'm sure they'll be thrilled to hear your voice."

Nina, touched by Dominic's words and overcome with emotion, leaned over to kiss him on the cheek. He tossed his long hair about, grinning from ear to ear as his eyes darted between the road and Nina.

"What was that for?" Nina sighed softly.

"Besides my parents, there aren't many people who are there for me. My PTSD and anxiety from my childhood still plague my life, but it seems like most people around me are sick and tired of hearing about it. It's sort of… heartwarming to have met you and have you listen to my story so patiently. It's the simple things that people I've known all my life don't even have time for. I'm grateful for you." Dominic looked down briefly as her words echoed through his mind. "Hey, if you want me to be your advocate, I don't mind."

"My advocate? How so?"

"However you want me to be." He winked and Nina rolled her eyes, not understanding what he was getting at. She appreciated the banter, anyway.

"Hey, if you want to be my advocate, go right ahead. My resort plans are canceled, I'm heading to yours. I mean, I'm completely at your mercy at this point."

Dominic cocked his eyes at her slyly.

"You make me sound like a serial killer or something. I won't hurt you!" Nina swallowed dramatically, glancing at the scenic views. Exotic birds glided in the sky, their majestic wings fluttering against the wind.

"Who knows, you could be!"

Dominic put a hand on his chest, feigning pain.

"Ouch, that hurts."

"Hey, you're a lawyer! I'm sure you've had harsher words said to you." He raised a finger at her, agreeing with her statement. "I can't argue with that!"

The two continued their journey, riding along on the road until they saw the sign for Onyx Resort, and headed in that direction. Thirty minutes later, they arrived at the sprawling venue, and the pair were stunned. Palm trees were everywhere; their massive leaves regally fluttering in the breeze.

"Wow!" Nina exclaimed as they parked their vehicle and retrieved their belongings from the trunk and walked into the open entryway of the brilliantly ornate, Onyx Renaissance Resort and Spa. They filled the interior with cream and gold accents, with the floor itself donning a rich, golden marble design. They kept it in an impeccable state. The sprawling oak reception counter was ornately designed, with multiple guest service agents scurrying about, assisting guests with their reservations. Dominic joined Nina in taking in the resort's lobby, astounded at the brilliant architecture. "This is something else, just unbelievable. I think I chose well." Nina rolled her eyes. "Of course you did, Mr. Advocate." She bit her lip as she followed him to reception. A kind-faced, heavyset woman greeted them with a warm smile, gesturing with her hands. "Hello, welcome to Onyx Resort, probably the best on the island! I'm Berna, and I'll be helping you check in this evening. I hope your flight was most enjoyable, coming in!" Nina shifted her eyes and Dominic stepped in with a ready answer. "It was lovely, we're both just tired, aren't we, Nina?" Happy he took the reins, she played along, exaggerating a yawn. "Exhausted. I'm just ready to tuck in for the night!" Nodding sympathetically, Berna turned back to Dominic.

"May I have the name on the reservation?"

"The name's Dominic McLeod. This is Nina, and she's not on the reservation, but I'd like her to be added immediately." Berna cleared her throat as she glanced Nina over, taking in her exasperated appearance. "Yes, sir, sure thing, right away." She typed away busily at the keyboard, glancing up at the pair every so often. "May I have your name, Miss?"

Dominic nodded, nudging Nina.

"Nina Saini."

"Thank you, ma'am. Let me just enter these details, and I'll go ahead and let you know the updated cost of your stay with us. It says here this is a one-week reservation. Would these details be staying the same?" Dominic glanced at his watch comically, as though he was going to find the answer there.

"Yes, one week. Nothing about my reservation changes except adding my companion to my room. It's a California King, that's what I paid for, you see all of that, right?" Nina looked down, smothering a smile. She could sense Dominic was becoming aggravated with Berna. *Feisty lawyer,* she thought shamefully. Thank God he couldn't hear her thoughts.

He shot a knowing look at her, and if he rolled his eyes back any further, they would have stayed that way permanently. Berna quickly typed, taking stock of the situation, and promptly handed Dominic two room keys and flashed the warmest smile she could muster, though her grin didn't meet her eyes.

"The elevators are down the corridor to your left, Mr. McLeod. You both will be in room 1506. We surely hope that you both have a restful, enjoyable stay in Turks and Caicos." She swiftly handed him an itinerary pamphlet. "We have plenty for you to do on the island. We recommend you take a look through this brochure and see if anything piques your interest!" Dominic winked and looked behind him, gesturing for Nina to follow. As though she was under his spell, she gave a half-smile to the front-desk attendant and shuffled beside Dominic, heading towards the elevators. Once there, he glanced around the hotel, appreciating the view.

"That woman was starting to annoy me. I don't get what's so hard for her to understand. My reservation was the same, except I was adding you to it! They make it seem like there's something else they need to investigate. I love to go on vacations, but I hate check-ins; it just takes too long." Nina smiled, looking down at the shiny marble floor as she clutched her suitcases.

"You know how it is, security issues and stuff. It's all protocol. I wouldn't sweat it!" The elevator dinged, and the pair entered. Dominic glanced at Nina through the elevator's interior mirrors, his eyes traveling over her body. Nina noticed, and she blushed but tried to hide it. "I guess you're not really used to people looking at you, huh?" Nina's fingers

traveled along with the grooved handle of her
luggage.

"Well, not really. I mean, some guys have been jerks
in the past. You know, catcalls and all that type of
stuff. I just don't buy into it. If a guy really wanted to
get to know me, he wouldn't have to do all that. Just
come up and talk to me like the woman I am."

Dominic placed a sympathetic hand on Nina's arm.
She wasn't used to men showing displays of affection
to her, and though it was foreign, Dominic's touch
felt different. She looked into his eyes as he gawked
at her, still feeling amazement that she was there with
him. The air in the elevator was heavy.

"I guess it's fair to say that I'm definitely on the right
track, right?"

The Island

The Glass Vine breakfast restaurant was bustling at 9:00 AM just as Nina and Dominic sauntered in. Eyeing each other knowingly and quickly each grabbed a plate, shuffling along the buffet line to gather their breakfast. Dominic's eyes traveled over Nina's body sensually. Her back was magnificently toned, and she couldn't have picked a better dress. She wore a halter, mustard-toned floral dress that showed off her back, hugged her curves, and flared at the hips. Dominic closed the space between them; Nina's butt grazing the front of his pants. She glanced back with a quizzical look on her face. Nina was digging into the scrambled eggs as she did so.

"You okay there, Dominic? You're a little close."

The lawyer placed a hand on Nina's hip, and she nearly sank into him from his tantalizing touch.

"That's kind of how I like it." He leaned forward, still gripping Nina as she slowly inched down the buffet line, ready to grab a croissant. Dominic rested his head near her ear, his hot breath stinging her neck in the best way. "And I think you kind of like it, too."

Nina rolled her eyes but allowed him to stay close to her. She felt oddly safe, though this was a man who she only had just met.

The night before had been a tad awkward, for obvious reasons.

There was a California King bed in the room, and though there was a sofa bed, Dominic insisted she should sleep on the bed with him. Donning an ivory slip that nearly made Dominic drop on his face when he saw her, he gestured to the bed as Nina stood on the opposite side, arms tightly crossed against her breasts.

"Nina, I don't bite. I wouldn't feel right about you sleeping on the sofa. What sort of man would I be?" Nina slowly uncrossed her arms, her perky breasts on full display as Dominic struggled to keep his eyes on her face. *Why is she teasing me like this?* He thought to himself as he shamefully trailed his eyes towards her shapely legs. He imagined what she was wearing underneath. The slip rested right above her knee, taunting the middle-aged lawyer as inappropriate thoughts invaded his mind. Nina's abundant hair hung loosely past her shoulders, shiny and strong.

I'd love to pull that hair into one and see what she'd do. Just grab her and... Nina cleared her throat loudly, repeating something Dominic had not heard. He shook his head at the naughty visions.

"I'm not questioning whether you'd do anything to me. It's just... well, you know! I'm sort of shy. I've never slept in a bed with another man before." Dominic gulped as he gawked at Nina, feeling zealous with that revelation.

"Well, if you're not going to sleep on the bed, I'll sleep on the sofa, okay? But I will not have a beautiful, amazing woman like yourself sleeping on a couch. I won't allow it! My priority is your comfort, so please, don't make this harder than it needs to be. Get on the bed." Smirking at the lawyer's firm yet sexy demands, Nina gestured her surrender, raising her hands above her head.

"Fine, fine! You win! I can see how successful you must be as a lawyer; very convincing." Nina maneuvered her way on the bed, her briefly open legs allowing Dominic to sneak a peek at her turquoise thong, scarcely covering her lady parts.

Dominic quickly looked away, fighting himself from devouring Nina right there. She gracefully adjusted the pillows behind her head, sitting back and fluttering her eyes, enjoying the comfort and coolness of the bed accessories. "This is wonderful. Cozy bed, plush pillows." She rubbed her hands across the smooth, burnt-tangerine toned duvet and tousled the ends of the sheet with her beautifully manicured toes, relishing in the nook. Dominic's eyes traveled across the landscape of Nina's incredibly sculpted body. He knew the thoughts in his head were wrong, but her beauty overcame him. Any man would fold.

After getting their breakfast, they chose a table towards the back of the busy restaurant, sitting adjacent to each other. Dominic donned a scrumptious grin as his hands ran through his silky, jet-black hair. The stubble on his face was in the right proportions; he looked handsome as the sun's rays from a nearby window illuminated his profile. Dominic looked damn-near ethereal. Nina squirmed in her seat.

"So, Dominic…" she paused, pondering about what to say. On one hand, she felt she shouldn't even be talking to this man. By chance, her airline seat was right next to his. She could have been anybody, but something had brought them together at that moment. On the other hand, it only felt natural to be right across from him, taking in his beautiful features. Dominic could feel Nina's palpating energy from across the table, and he only wished he could reach for her hand, clasping them firmly between his, but he restrained himself. He wanted to hear what she had to say. Attempting to remain stoic, he dug into his breakfast, though never breaking eye contact with Nina. He didn't want to miss a thing.

"Family law, huh? It definitely sounds intense."

Dominic cocked his head back, struggling to chew the eggs in his mouth. "Oh yeah, it definitely can be. Lots of tears, fraught with anger. It's weird though, because I love being in the middle of it." Nina smirked, sipping on her coffee. "You live for the drama, huh?"

"Drama? Well, I guess you can say that. I don't find anything funny about a family breaking down, but I'm definitely focused and ready to resolve matters right away. The sooner, the better. The worst cases I've worked on were the ones that were dragged out. Tensions are high, lots of crying and stress. Sometimes, the couples decide to rescind the proceedings, in hopes of reconciliation. A month down the line, someone refiles with the court. It's a lot, but I live for this. I'm the first lawyer in my family, so it was a big thing when I passed the bar. It seems like everyone thought I'd get into criminal law, but it's just not my thing." Nina played with her fingers as she watched the handsome Dominic closely. She hoped she wasn't making it too obvious that she was staring at his lips.

"Well, kudos to you. It's always awesome when you're the first in the family to achieve something amazing. I bet some of them ask you for free legal advice." Dom rolled his eyes, recalling in his mind the many times where this occurred. "Yeah, they do from time to time. I've gotten mostly harmless requests; where does my property line start? Can I sue my neighbor for their dog peeing on my lawn, things like that?" Nina giggled, almost choking on her food.

"Well! That's something else. But you know what? Good for you! Lawyers have a tough job, no matter what their specialty might be. You probably have a great team of lawyers you work with and rely on for successful trials, right?" Dominic slightly shrugged his shoulders, as though there was only some truth to her question. "Well, I mean, I do have a few good lawyers that I work alongside. They are sufficient, but I wouldn't mind a few improvements on their end. Though we all work on different cases, we're a part of the same team, so a sense of uniformity is something I often seek, but rarely ever get. You know, I like to come into work clean-shaven; well-groomed. It's expected that fellow lawyers would do the same, but they hardly ever do."

"Yeah? What do you mean?" Nina inquired, curious.

Dominic raised the side of his mouth, considering how to word his statements.

"We're buddies, you know? We go out when we have some downtime from our cases. Hit up a few bars and restaurants, dress real casual. We hardly look like attorneys when we're on the town. But during these off-time hangouts, I try to hint to these guys that they need to tighten up the hatches, you know? Present themselves a little better around the office and when they're in court. They think I'm just being an ass, but appearances are very important in this industry. An attorney who doesn't look put together is frowned upon, and they will lack tact and a presence in the courtroom as they fight for their clients. I'm just trying to look out for them, but they see it as me trying to one-up them." Nina wiped her mouth as she finished her last bite, putting her plate to the side of the table to be collected by the wait staff.

"Do you think that perhaps you have unreasonable demands? I mean, you're an attorney, just as the rest of them are. Maybe they are taking offense because you are all on the same mission, to fight for your clients to get the best possible results. How they want to dress is how they wish to present themselves. I know you probably have the best intentions; there's no question about that, but at the same time, the lines will become blurred as you, on one hand, fight desperately for your clients, but try to essentially client your colleagues. Do you see what I mean? I don't mean to insult you." Dominic licked his chops as the brilliant lady in front of him looked off to the side, donning an embarrassed look she tried to conceal. Her cheeks blushed, and she pressed her lips together, as though she felt like she said too much. Dominic was using all his composure to prevent himself from grabbing her from across the table and plopping her into his lap.

"I totally get what you mean, and believe me, no offense taken. I want to know everything I can about you. There's just something I can feel deep in me that I want to explore. I know that probably sounds like a script. I mean, give me a break. You're talking to a lawyer. We don't really go up there and wing it." Nina burst out in laughter, thankful that the restaurant was loud enough that she didn't draw attention to herself. Tucking her hair behind her ear, Dominic pointed out something he hadn't seen before.

"Nina, is that a tattoo that I see? Right there, behind your ear?" Nina turned back to face him, giggling as she traced the tattoo with her finger, as though she forgot she had it.

"Yeah, it's nothing. Just my zodiac sign."

Dominic cocked his head, looking closely as Nina turned her own to give him a better look."

"Ah, so you're a Cancer, huh?"

"Yup! Emotional, intuitive, home-body type of gal. That's me!"

Dominic, this time, reached across the table and held Nina's warm hand into his, and gently ran his thumb against her smooth skin.

"And beautiful, and smart, and kind. Don't forget all those things." Nina blushed; her sparkly white teeth glistened from the rays bouncing off Dominic's shoulders. "Well, thank you. So, what's your Zodiac?" Dominic dusted off his shoulders dramatically, causing Nina to roll her eyes as she bit back laughter. "I'm a Scorpio. November 2. I guess it would make sense why people think I'm super intense. They tend to say that a lot. Do you think I am?" Nina shrugged her shoulders, unable to stifle her giggles anymore. She felt so silly, so light at that moment. "Well, to be honest, you are pretty intense, but in a good way. I'm not saying that to hurt your feelings or anything. I can tell you're very smart as well. And of course…" she trailed off and slowly drew her hand away from Dominic's, instead, rubbing them together. Dominic cocked his head at her, quizzically. "And of course what, Nina? What were you going to say?" He bit his lip as he stared at her. She looked so *good* in that dress.

"Well, of course, you're handsome, too. But I'm sure you get that a lot. You probably defend a lot of scorned women who would love to get a chance to be with you if you weren't assisting them in a legal matter." Dominic sat back, surprised by Nina's unusually bold statement, in contrast to the immense shyness she had been displaying.

"Well, you're right, I do defend lots of women, and I'd be lying if I said none of them were physically attractive. But I can assure you, my job at hand overrode any sensual feelings I might have had. I don't seduce the women that call my office, hoping to start divorce proceedings. There's a job to be done, at all times. Staying professional is what I'm all about."

Nina narrowed her eyes surreptitiously at Dominic.

"I guess you just seduce the ladies you meet up with at the airport then, huh?"

Dominic laughed out loud, quickly tapping his fingers on the table in nervousness.

"You're the most beautiful lady I've ever laid eyes on. So no, that's not what I do."

Nina cleared her throat as a strong breeze entered through a double door that has been propped open. She rubbed her shoulders and Dominic followed her gaze knowingly.

"I think we've been in here long enough. The morning's still going strong. What do you want to do first, go to the beach?" Nina nodded incessantly, wanting to get out of the sexually tense situation.

"Yeah, let's go." They stood up simultaneously and as per normal, Dominic held Nina by the waist and led them out of the busy restaurant, dodging children who were running about with full plates in their hands.

Dominic flashed a smile as a young boy whizzed past, juice nearly spilling from his cup.

"Kids, huh? You've gotta love them!"

"Yeah, you're telling me!"

The pair quickly made their way back to their hotel room and put on their swimsuits. Dominic's jaw almost dropped to the floor as he took in Nina's one-piece white bathing suit. It had an open back and sides, and a low-cut front that teased him to no end. There were gold chain designs on the front of the swimsuit. Nina looked stunning. "Wow!" Dominic made sizzling noises as Nina laughed, cautiously looking at herself in the floor-length mirror to make sure nothing was out of place. "Do you think I look okay?" Dom's eyes widened. "Okay? Just okay? Nina!" he exclaimed as he positioned his buff body behind hers. Standing at 6'2, he easily towered over her 5'6 frame and hesitantly placed his hand around her waist, finally resting on her trim stomach.

"You have an unbelievable body. Do you exercise?"

Nina shook her head as she nervously pondered where to place her arms. Dominic's stance hindered a lot of options. "Not really, no. But I do a lot of yoga, so that could be it! Lots of planks, different poses."

She stepped away from Dominic briefly, and without provocation, performed a full split on the floor, causing Dominic to stammer back, stunned.

"Ta-da! Oh, I guess I didn't tell you, but I also took gymnastics as a child, so I can still do this." She gave jazz hands and giggled as Dominic gawked at her, not really knowing how to react to Nina being in such a compromising position.

"I mean... what can I say? Shy but talented. I dig it! You are unbelievable." Hesitantly helping her to her feet, as he really would have loved to see how long she could hold the pose, Nina wiped her buttocks briskly and adjusted her swimsuit around her legs as Dom watched her closely in the mirror, unable to hide his excitement. If they didn't leave, it was going to be a very different scene in that room.

"Let's head out." He murmured huskily, ushering her out of the room and out of the resort hotel.

It was almost noon, and the sun beat down on the pair as they traversed down the incredible stretch of white sand. Nina, with her hair now in a tight ponytail, shielded her eyes as she watched paragliders out on the open sea, enjoying the sun's rays and crystal-clear water. Many people were swimming and playing beach volleyball. A comforting breeze trickled across Nina's shoulders, and she felt oddly confident as she walked beside the sexy lawyer, who seemed to be always keeping a close eye on her.

"So, tell me about you, Nina. I feel like I've been talking so much about myself. I'd love to get to know you a bit more. You're doing photography, so how's that been going for you?" Nina ran her hands against her thighs as the breeze tossed her ponytail about. "Yeah, I'm big on photography. I love to take pictures of just about everything. I guess about the only time I don't have my camera gear is right now, but that's for the wedding tomorrow."

Dom put his arm around her, wanting to know more.

"Wait, did you hear from your clients since you've been here? Are they staying at the resort you were supposed to go to?" Nina groaned as she nodded her head. "Yup, they are over there. I actually got an email from the bride this morning. I told her about my change of accommodations but reassured her I'd be there bright and early tomorrow for the wedding. She did sound nervous, so I had to reiterate a few times that nothing about our agreement had changed. I understand though, as I'm the photographer for such a monumental occasion. She just wanted to make sure everything would run smoothly." Dom drew in a sharp breath, worried that he may have complicated matters by asking Nina to join him at his resort. He threw a lifeline.

"Well, you know I'm going to be here for you on this entire trip, no matter what. I'll drive you over to the resort tomorrow and I'll stay with you until your job's done, no questions asked." Nina protested, raising her hand in the air. "No, trust me, that won't be necessary. You've done enough kind things for me, like paying for my stay with you… me, someone you've only met just a short time ago! I can't make you accompany me on a work job, especially because you're here on vacation! It would be so wrong of me." Dom stopped in his tracks and lifted Nina's chin; a serious look spread across his face.

"Listen, if I want to do something nice for the most beautiful lady in the world, I'll do it, and there's nothing that you can do to stop me. I feel like this is partially my fault; I took you away from your plans, not thinking about how it would have affected your job. No matter the implications, I'm going to make

things right. Anything you want, consider it done."
Feeling as though she couldn't refuse, Nina placed
her hand delicately on Dom's arms as she looked up
at him, squinting because the sun was directly
beaming into her eyes. "Alright, Dominic, if you
insist. I won't protest against it any longer." Smiling
widely, Dom looked around, searching for what to
say next. "In that case…" he trailed off as he abruptly
lifted Nina off the ground and dashed towards the
water like a madman.

She erupted into a fit of laughter as she lightly tapped
on his back. "Hey, stop! Let me go! What are you
doing, Dominic?!" She felt his body heave with
excitement as he clutched firmly on her behind, not
wanting her to fall off.
"Your case is weak, Nina!"

"You've got everything, right?" Dom inquired as he watched Nina briskly walk around the massive hotel suite, gathering her photography equipment. It was 8:00 AM and the wedding was due to start at 1 PM. They ordered room service an hour before, enjoying a light continental breakfast with hot coffee and tea.

She had to get to the resort early to take makeup shots of the bride and her wedding party. Despite the warm climate, Nina decided on black straight-leg trousers, a matching blazer with a gray fooler top attached, and heavily embellished ballet flats. The trousers showed off her incredible behind enticingly.

"Yeah, I think so…" she trailed off, halting her movement as her eyes quickly scanned the room. Her eyes rested on Dominic, who had been glaring at her for some time. "Scratch that, Dominic. You're not a bit intense. You're *very* intense. Is this what you normally do? Stare aimlessly? Hopelessly, even?"

Dominic nearly fell over, laughing as he reached over to tickle Nina. She yelped, her eyes widening at the sensation. "Dominic!" He raised his hands, surrendering. "Okay, alright. Listen, I can't help myself. You're just so beautiful, I can't keep my hands off of you." Nina scoffed. "Well, you're going to have to try if you're coming along for the ride, you know? I have to have full concentration. I have about four grand riding on this shoot. It's a wedding, after all. They already have so much to worry about. I wouldn't want to be one of those things." Lifting some of her equipment, Dominic smiled sweetly.

"Let me help you out! I don't want you to think that I'm this sort of sleazy, no-good lawyer that likes to touch you. There's more to me than just that, trust me!" Heading towards the door, Nina held it open with her free hand to let Dominic through.

"Oh Dominic, I'm starting to see that you can be quite dramatic, and I thought I was!" The duo headed out of the resort and packed up the car, hitting the road at a strong speed as a delightful breeze rippled through the cabin of the vehicle.

Nina propped her arm up against the passenger door frame as she breathed in the tropical air, sort of wishing she didn't have to wear full black attire. It was industry practice, however, and it helped to draw attention away from herself, and better blend in with the crowd as she worked. Dominic cleared his throat as his powerful hands gripped the wheel.

"I know this might be a sensitive topic, and you don't have to go into details if you don't want to but, how did your phobia come about? You know, your fear of flying?" Feeling a bit anxious, Nina rubbed her hands together. She didn't want to delve into specifics, but Dominic was being extremely accommodating, so she owed it to him to open up more about her experiences. "Well, I had a really unpleasant encounter on a plane when I was traveling to England with my parents. Believe it or not, I used to be in the skies more than I was on the ground, it seemed. It was just surreal. I just can't believe I'm here right now."

Dom nodded quietly, trying to focus on the road. "So what happened on the plane that day? How did it lead to this?"

"Turbulence. A severe case of it, too. The entire plane was rocking and thrashing about. I was just a teen, so I tried to stay calm, but I was quickly losing control. Oh gosh, and then a guy threw up. It was loud and absolute chaos! I wish I could forget that day." Nina rubbed her temples, remembering how frightened she was. Dominic sighed, feeling guilt ripple through him. *I just keep asking the wrong thing,* he thought in his head, biting back words.

"Listen, I'm sorry. I keep fucking up and putting you in compromising positions. I'll shut up and never talk about it again. You know, you'd think for a lawyer, I'd know when to stop talking and read the room!"

Nina groaned, though her chest rose and fell with laughter as she leaned against the door, allowing the breeze to invade her face. She knew she couldn't be upset with Dominic. "No, listen! You're doing all the right things, and I feel like I'm messing up the entire mood! I sort of get emotional about my phobia, and sometimes when I recall that day, I get shivers down my spine."

"No, I can't help but feel like I'm saying all the wrong things."

"Pull over, Dom. Pull over."

Arching his back in his seat, Dominic listened to her demand and pulled off to the shoulder, worry spread across his face as he watched Nina intently.

Nina placed her hand on Dominic's thigh, and he watched her wide-eyed as her lips began to move.

"I'm sorry. You're doing so many nice things to me, and I'm being so standoffish. Like, look! You're taking me to my job site and it's just friendly gesture after friendly gesture. I'm so embarrassed." She began to massage his thigh unknowingly, and Dominic sat back in his chair, enjoying the sudden show of affection. "It's okay, Nina. No worries. We should try to get back on the road as soon as possible. I wouldn't want you to be late for your job."

Nina leaned in and kissed Dominic softly on the lips, before sitting back and keeping her gaze on the road ahead. A smile spread across her face as she saw Dominic's mouth quiver with emotion. He covered the front of his pants as he peeled out of the shoulder and sped down the road, feeling like John Travolta in Grease. "Damn! Nina! You're hot and cold, huh?"

Nina gagged, toying with her ponytail. "I guess so!"

After a while, the two arrived at Ivory Shores Resort, a quaint strip of the island not as prestigious and grand as the Onyx, but still respectable. A pair of women danced about with coconuts in their hands, lovely, upbeat music playing in the distance.

"Cute," Dominic stated flatly as Nina flashed a sarcastic look. They disembarked from the vehicle and gathered the photography equipment, and headed into the main lobby of the small resort.

"Hey now, you've gotta give an E for effort."

"Yeah, okay." He pointed out cobwebs in the corners of the lobby's revolving door. "Effort my ass. I think it's a good idea you're not spending any extended amount of time here. Let's head to the lobby and solve some issues, shall we? Did you end up calling them to cancel your reservation?"

Nina gulped.

"Well, I did give them a quick call, but they said I'd have to pay a grand for cancellation fees." Dominic cocked his head back as they sauntered to the front desk. It was surprisingly quiet, the time approaching 9:00 AM. A restaurant attached to the lobby had a few patrons, some enjoying light refreshments and hot beverages. A wondrous breeze flew through open windows above the reception desk.

"Dom, please. Just sit here, and I'll deal with it. It wasn't your reservation, anyway. Let me handle it."

Dominic stopped in his tracks, the tripod bag nearly falling out of his hand.

"Listen, Nina. I'm not going to let anyone take advantage of you if I have anything to do with it. You're too damn polite to people! I know it's your nature, and I like how you are. Believe me, I've never done this for anyone else. I want you to have the most enjoyable time here, despite me not wanting to be

here for another second." He gazed disapprovingly
around the open-concept lobby, not pleased with the
layout or state of the architecture.

"No matter what, though, I'm staying here until the
wedding is over." Nina raised her hand in protest.

"Dominic, no. Please. Just hand me my things, wait in
the car, and let me find the wedding party. I won't be
here all night; the wedding starts at 1:00 PM and it's a
cocktail-style setup. Not much to it, honestly. I might
not even get a break in between. I have just enough
time to do a quick briefing with the wedding party
before I have to get started."

Dominic rested a hand on her shoulder.

"Let's go." Nina groaned as the lawyer led the way,
once again. She was starting to wonder if this was
why his coworkers were critical of him. He definitely
enjoyed being in charge. Determination was his
middle name, and he wore it well.

The pair approached the desk where a middle-aged
man whose uniform shirt was a tad big forced a smile
as he looked on at them, fingers on the keyboard at
the ready. "Good morning, welcome to Ivory Shores
Resort. We are pleased to help you today with a
smooth check-in. May I have the name of the person
on the reservation?"

"Um, Nina…" she started to say before Dominic
intervened. "Nina Saini. She was supposed to check
in here, on Thursday, but she's staying at another
resort but is here for work. Photographer for a

wedding that you have booked." Eyes dodging between Nina and Dominic, the man quickly entered the details into the computer and placed a finger on his chin thoughtfully.

"Oh yes, Ms. Saini. Yes, we have successfully canceled your reservation with us. We regret you had to do so, but we understand that things do come up. I see…" he trailed off, going over the details.

"I see you were, unfortunately, charged cancellation fees to the sum of one-thousand dollars. We automatically charged it to the credit card we have on file. We understand that you are here for a photography job for a wedding for Mr. and Ms. Cain. Will you still be doing this today?"

"Ah…"

"Yes, she will be. Nina will be meeting with her clients in a moment, so we'll have to sort these matters out immediately." Dominic took a firm stance, his fist resting on the counter. "Can we have those cancellation fees revoked this time, please? This is a unique circumstance. Something came up, as you said yourself, things happen! How about it?"

The attendant shook his head, rubbing his hands together defiantly.

"Oh no, I'm sorry, Sir. We don't have that capability and we're very clear about the fees we impose. But, if you are both traveling together and will be here for most of the morning and afternoon, you're free to lounge around in the restaurant and, as an extra

gesture for the unique circumstances here, all meals
will be on us. Will this suffice?"

Nina nodded, in full agreement with the receptionist
as Dominic pondered about his offer, though a sense
of dissatisfaction lingered on his face. He reached
into his back pocket and pulled out wads of cash.
Nina and the attendant's eyes widened as Dominic
began counting the cash in front of them until he
reached one thousand. Rolling the cash in a rubber
band, he handed it to Nina, clasping her hand over it.

"Put that on your credit card. I think *that suffices*." He
cut his eyes at the man behind the counter as he
gestured for Nina to follow him to the restaurant's
tables. Nina dragged her feet, embarrassed to meet
the eyes of the hotel staff as she took a seat across
Dominic, who had a proud look on his face.

She exhaled sharply, trying to keep herself composed
as she eyed the watch on her wrist.

"Dominic, you didn't have to do all that! Listen, I
know that you're a lawyer and you're used to
standing up for people, and even for yourself! But
please, must you exert this everywhere you go? The
man looked like he was about to shit himself."

Dominic flashed a smug grin as he looked over her
shoulder and at the man at the counter, who had been
peering over at them curiously.

"Nah, he could have refunded you the money,
especially because you're here right now on a work

assignment. He's just being an asshole, and I'm not
going to let anyone take advantage of your kindness."

Nina stood up, grabbed the gear from Dom's hands,
and struck a defiant pose. Dominic felt the hair stand
up on his neck as he admired his newfound friend's
body. It was incredible how even while annoyed; she
looked even more beautiful.

"Okay, so you're probably mad at me. But I can't
help it, okay? Listen, go, and find your clients, and
I'll be right here, okay? It doesn't matter how long it
takes; I'll be here waiting for you until it's time to
head back to Onyx. Alright? Please, just don't look at
me like that." Nina stifled a grin as she shuffled
towards the door with her camera gear, looking back
at Dominic as she swayed her hips. He licked his
chops as he watched her leave.

"You better be right here when I come back; no funny
business, Dominic."

Stopping outside of the lobby to look down at her
phone, Nina made her way to one of the resort's hotel
buildings and arrived on the third floor, knocking on
room 312. Swiftly, the door opened and a short, stout
woman with makeup that looked overdone stood
before Nina, her brows fraught but a smile displayed.

"Hi, you're the photographer, right? Nina, is it?"

"Yes, that's me! I hope I'm not too late."

"Oh no, right on time, right on time, honey! Wow,
you're pretty! Lovely, great! Okay, come on in, the

bride's just finishing up her makeup, let's get a few shots in before we get this party started! Oh, by the way, I'm the maid of honor, Bethany. I'm sort of, well, you know, making sure everything runs smoothly for the bride." She leaned in for a whisper.

"Don't take it to heart, but the bride's a bit flustered today. You know how it is, jitters and what have you. The groom… ugh, don't get me started. Never really liked the jerk anyway, but let's just keep that between you and me." Nina gave a nervous smile as the animated woman moved about the modestly sized hotel suite. Nina closed the door behind her and looked around the rather unexciting room, spotting the bride sitting at the vanity, her hair in a lovely updo.

"Hi, I'm Nina! The photographer! Jamie, right? You look absolutely lovely!" She approached the woman hesitantly, so as not to aggravate her. Jamie dabbed at her eyes, signaling she had been crying but trying to hide it. She had dark auburn hair, and a tiara rested atop her head. It appeared her makeup had been expertly done but was now blotched because of tears. The woman's abundant eyelashes fluttered as she glared at Nina up and down, letting out a sharp breath.

"Finally, you're here." She started, taking a deep breath and repositioning herself on the chair. "Sorry, let's try that again. Nice to meet you, Nina. Let's get this over with. How about you do a few shots of me staring at myself in the mirror? My idiot soon-to-be husband is nowhere to be found, probably got plastered with the groomsmen and now stumbling somewhere on this ridiculous property. I don't even know why he chose this place; it sucks. We should have gone to the Onyx; They had way better reviews." Nina bit back as she drew her camera out and pointed it at the frustrated bride-to-be, trying to capture the perfect image. The bride cocked her head in various positions, but none of them looked natural. It was clear she was in distress, and not getting into the groove of taking pictures. Nina stood back and looked at the shots she had snapped, thinking of a way to inspire Jamie. "Have you had a drink yet, Jamie? It's your wedding day! How about we fix you a mimosa? I'm sure you've had a stressful morning. Have you eaten?" Nina gestured to a table full of champagne and juices, along with boiled eggs, croissants, mixed fruits, and an assortment of cheeses.

"No, I didn't eat, I mean how can I? Jasper is nowhere to be found, I'm all alone, my bridesmaids aren't good for anything, I'm just done with all of this!" Jamie tossed a beauty blended towards the vanity mirror, a smudge left behind on the glass.

Nina took slow breaths and looked behind her, as Bethany and two other women, presumably Jamie's bridesmaids, cowered toward the back of the room, clearly afraid to add fuel to the fire. Nina turned to Jamie and stroked her back, attempting to soothe the distressed woman.

"Listen, I see this a lot, and I understand how it can be. It's difficult. Both you and your husband have quite a bit on your plate. Traveling to Turks and Caicos, I mean wow! Having a wedding overseas was probably difficult to orchestrate. I mean, I can only imagine, right? I got a few good shots, so how about you grab a bite, and just enjoy the moment for now? While you eat, I'll take a few shots of the food, okay?" Jamie sat back quietly, obviously trying to compose herself and consider Nina's requests.

"You know what? You are right. I'm the bride, and I should enjoy this time. Fuck Jasper. I'm going to eat and relax. Seems like the photographer knows more about me than my own friends do." Jamie cut daggers at her wedding party as she sauntered to the food table, grabbing a plate and helping herself. Nina bit back comments as she grabbed her trusty camera and began taking shots of the food and the bride's back profile, taking notice of her stunning wedding dress. It had a short train, but impressive embroidery embellished the spectacular gown.

"I've got to say, Jamie. This has to be the most beautiful dress I've ever seen!" Jamie looked back at Nina with a champagne glass in her hand, and Nina thought in that split moment, it would make the perfect picture. "Hold that pose, Jamie."

Nina took a few steps back, appreciating the sun's rays trickling in through the massive windows in the room. As if on cue, Bethany opened the balcony door, letting in a powerful gust of warm, tropical air. The breeze enveloped the bride-to-be, still clasping tightly onto her glass of bubbly, and gave her the most genuine smile as Nina captured a breathtaking shot. Almost giddy, Nina approached Jamie and showed her the picture. Her look softened as she down the last of her champagne, grinning approvingly at Nina.

"That is a lovely shot. The prettiest I've looked for a long while. Lovely, just lovely."

She gobbled a few chunks of cantaloupe and carefully dabbed at her thin lips, looking around the room.

"It's a small thing we're having, you know. Real small gathering. Never did we think we'd be having a vacation in the Caribbean, but here we are, right? I'm telling you; you'd think it'd be a happy day, right? And I'm trying to be, I'm trying my best, but my damn groom isn't anywhere to be found, and it's coming close to ceremony time."

Nina looked at her watch, which read 11:00 AM.

"Where is Jasper now? It would be great to get some shots of him and you before we head out to the beach, right? Is there a way to phone him?"

Right then, the door flew open and a man with a buzz cut and the body of a college footballer sauntered in, half stumbling with a clean black suit on, void of a tie or undershirt. "Hi baby, happy wedding day," he muttered as he wrapped his arms around Nina, his hands firmly clutching her waist. Nina's cheeks swiftly reddening as she retreated from the intoxicated groom, putting her hand to her mouth in disbelief. Embarrassed and annoyed, Jamie shoved Jasper hard in the chest. "Jas, I'm right here, you dick! This is the photographer, Nina. You are an absolute moron; can you get your shit together? What the hell are you doing? Where's your tie and white-collared shirt? Are you kidding me right now?" Bethany and the other bridesmaids quickly headed onto the balcony, not wanting to be a part of the situation.

Jasper, shockingly handsome with his dimpled chin, but clearly in over his head, pointed aimlessly at Nina, looking at her up and down, eyes glazed over. "You're the hottest photographer I have ever seen in my life. No seriously, wow!" Nina shifted her feet uncomfortably, looking down at the floor as she thought of what to say. Jamie stepped in.

"Jasper! Listen to me, listen! I'm your wife-to-be. We're about to get married. Can we get it together, please? This isn't okay! You're going to scare off our photographer. She's here, and we're paying her big money. Did you forget she had an airplane phobia that she had to beat just to come here? That's correct, right?" she cocked her head at Nina, awaiting confirmation. Nina winced at the blatancy of her question, but she remained professional.

"Well, yes. That is true, but this isn't about me; I'm here to support you all, no matter what. How about we take a few pics of you guys in the room? Then we'll head over to the beach. Is everything already set up over there?" Jamie twisted what Nina assumed to be her engagement ring around her finger gingerly.

"Yep, all set up. You're right. Let's take a few shots and head out. Wait!" She marched over to the balcony and swung the doors open, ready to sink her teeth into her wedding party.

"Hey, wedding party, hiding out here, huh? Luckily, this nice photographer is prepared and ready to go.

Head over to the beach and make sure everything is ready, alright? Make yourselves useful." She spat as the women shuffled from the balcony and sauntered past the drunk groom-to-be, who passingly raised his hand to them in some form of odd acknowledgment.

"Looking wonderful ladies! Bethany, the ass on you, my god!" Nina stood there, mouth ajar as Jasper gawked at the maid of honor's behind. She turned red as a beet as she followed the other women out of the room. Jamie looked deeply embarrassed.

Why are they getting married if the groom can't even focus on his own bride? Yikes, Nina thought as she brought the camera up, pointing at the couple.

"Wait, pretty photographer, don't I need a prop or something? I want to make your job easier for you." He grabbed a full bottle of champagne off of the food table behind him, and held it in front of him, as though it was his weapon of choice.

"Jasper, put the bottle down!" Jamie demanded, looking at Nina for moral support. She tried a different angle to get the ball moving. "Hold on, Jamie, this is making for a great picture. Hold that pose, Jasper; you both are looking exceptional." Through his drunken stupor, a flash of boldness entered the groom's eyes, as he firmly gripped Jamie's waist and struck a strong pose for the camera. Nina snapped multiple shots, many of which were sexual in nature. In one, Jasper forcefully turned Jamie away from him, so that her behind was grazing his front. He grabbed her breast and donned a smug expression.

"How about this?" Without missing a beat and not wanting to stay in the hotel suite any longer, she snapped the sexual picture and summoned the couple to her, showing her the array of shots she had taken. Jasper popped the cork off the champagne and took a large swig straight from the bottle, much to their dismay. "Oh, you're good. You're really good. Honey, you did such a good job picking a photographer. This may be our best wedding yet!" Nina smirked as Jamie rolled her eyes.

"It's our only wedding, dick! You know what, less talking, more going to the beach, am I right? Let's go. Come, Nina, let's go." Obediently, she grabbed the rest of her gear as Jasper staggered about, finally getting a hold of the doorknob. "Nina goes first. She's the real MVP here." Nina almost rolled her eyes as she headed out of the room. She stood at the elevator, waiting for the couple as they struggled to close the suite door. *Let's just get to the beach, people!* She thought to herself. *Such a dysfunctional couple.*

They reserved a small stretch of beach for the wedding party, and only eight chairs with organza bows lined the white sand. Two tables stood stationary close by, beautifully adorned with pink, sea-green, and silver décor. A longer rectangle table stood opposite the round ones, filled with hot trays of appetizers as well as fruit and cheese platters. Nina, waddling in the sand, adamant about not getting any in her shoes, looked at Bethany curiously, gesturing to the seats.

"Is that it? It's just you guys? No moms, dads? Cousins?" Bethany sighed, crossing her arms across her ample stomach. "Unfortunately, not everyone could afford to come to the island and partake in the wedding." She inched forward to whisper, something she seemed to do a lot of.

"But between you and me, the most probable reason is that the bride and groom's union…. Well… you've seen just a glimpse for yourself. He's a hottie, there's no question. I mean, look at him!" She gestured to Jasper, who stood at the flower arch, adjusting his black jacket nervously. He still had on no tie or undershirt. Bethany continued.

"Despite his good looks, he's an ass. He hits on women in front of Jamie all the time. At first, she used to tell him how she felt about it, but now, she just accepts it. He has even *cheated* on her. So gross. We've tried fruitlessly to stop her from marrying this guy, but she was sure that she could change him by tying the knot. Clearly, that doesn't seem to be working. You're a beautiful woman; I wouldn't be surprised if he's already made passes on you!" Nina bit her lip, not wanting to diverge information on the matter. Bethany nodded firmly, Nina's silence proving her point.

"You don't even have to answer that, because we all know how he is. He's hit on me, and all the other women in Jamie's life. But what can we do, right? All we've tried to do is show Jamie support, even if we think she's making a huge mistake. Love is love, and unfortunately, it seems like my best friend is blinded by it. This right here…" she pointed subtlety between Jasper and Jamie, who stood adjacent to one another, inelegantly looking at the sea before them.

"This isn't love, plain and simple. Just don't tell them I told you that."

Bethany patted Nina's shoulder and made her way to the altar as she fumbled with the camera in her hands. Deciding to make the most of the situation, she began taking stunning shots of the setup, with the backdrop of the water offering a calm aura to a very real, tense situation. A man in a robe who was clearly a minister of some kind walked to the altar with papers and a book in his hand.

"Are we ready? Can we start the ceremony?" Fanning her face, Jamie nodded incessantly, eager to get things over with. "Please, Paul. Let's get er done."

Clearing his throat with Nina at the ready with her camera, the minister spoke.

"We are gathered here today, on the beautiful island of Turks and Caicos, to witness the union of Jamie and Jasper. These two met in college, and ever since then, they've been tied to one another in the best ways possible." The shortest, petite bridesmaid cleared her throat, clearly not agreeing with the minister's sentiments. Jamie cringed as she held Jasper's hands. He was still swaying as residual alcohol ran through his system. Nina snapped a few zoomed-in shots, frowning upon inspecting them afterward. The couple looked despondent and uninterested in one another, with Jamie particularly glum. It was proving difficult to capture beautiful moments when the couple was so disconnected from each other. Photos of the bridesmaids turned out superbly, with the women donning fresh smiles full of hope and rejuvenation. *They are a quirky bunch, but they're trying,* Nina thought to herself, getting behind the last woman to capture an angled shot.

Jamie tapped her feet impatiently as the pastor finished his sentiments. He seemed unfazed by the glaringly obvious divide between the pair.

"By the power invested in me, I now pronounce you husband and wife." He turned to Jasper.

"You may now kiss the bride." Eyes now agile and wide, Jasper smothered Jamie, planting wet kisses all over her face. Bethany placed a finger atop her lip, smirking as she looked down at the sand beneath her feet. "Thank you, pastor, thank you! Praise the Lord! And thank you!" He pointed directly at Nina, who held the camera in her hands and was about to snap a shot. Her eyes widened as she saw Jasper charging toward her, arms out and mouth puckered as if he wanted to kiss her. Nervously, she dodged him in the nick of time, causing Jasper to stumble and almost lose his footing. Whipping around, he pointed his finger jokingly, gawking at Nina as his eyes trailed up and down her body. "You're a sneaky photographer, aren't you? Sexy too…" Nina spun on her heels and almost bumped into Jamie, who was blushing incessantly and rubbing her temples.

"Listen, Nina. I'm sorry for all of this. My husband is a jerk! I can't even imagine what you must be thinking right now; I'm so embarrassed. Listen, I'm sure you've got enough shots and…" Bethany shrieked as Jasper tumbled into a food table, knocking over an entire plate of appetizers into the sand. "Fucks sake. Listen, Nina. I think your work here is done. This is so wrong, on so many levels. I know I convinced you to come here, and I'm sure you were expecting far better than this. Trust me, I know I was. Listen, when you have a chance, send me the photos you've already taken, that'll have to do. There's nothing left for you to take pictures of. Jasper is an absolute snob that has no respect for the people around him. You probably are wondering why I even married him, but that's a story better left untold. Thank you for everything; for putting up with this. I'll be sure to give you a good rating because I don't think any other photographer would have put up with this. Feel free, uh…" she gestured to the food table, where Jasper was still staggering about, eating chicken on a skewer. "Feel free to grab some food on your way. All the best, thank you again." The woman lightly tapped Nina's shoulder and held the train of her dress, waddling towards her wedding party.

"Wow. I cannot believe all of that just happened." She muttered to herself as she scrambled around the area, collecting her equipment. After gathering her stuff, she headed straight for the lobby and instantly spotted Dominic, who was sipping a hot beverage.

As though he sensed her coming, he looked up, flashing a cheeky smile, and headed straight for Nina, relieving her of the bags in her hand. Dominic gave Nina a quick peck on the cheek, and Nina hung her head, feeling fatigue run through her. Dominic noted her meek demeanor, concern growing on his face. "Wow, was it that bad?"

"Let's go, now!"

She shuffled towards the door, and Dominic followed close behind, prying for answers.

"You've been working for a while, though! Don't want to grab some food before we go?" Nina shot him a deathly look, and he recoiled, leading her straight to the rental vehicle. They piled in and shot out of the parking lot like a rocket, and for the first time since she arrived, a genuine smile spread across her face. Dominic looked at her periodically, a quizzical yet comical glare painted on his face.

"You look like you could use a drink."

"I'm not joking, man; it was that crazy! The man was all over me and stuff, it made me feel really uncomfortable." Nina moaned as Dominic poured himself a shot of whisky, offering her one. She happily accepted, downing it before Dominic had a chance to make a toast.

"Let me get this straight. You're there to shoot a wedding, and the groom is all over you like that? I mean, that gets me really pissed off. Maybe it's the lawyer in me. I wish I would have been there, and we would have seen if he had the guts to put his hands on you." The pair sat in their hotel suite, lounging on the plush mahogany sofa bed.

Nina wore the same pants but ditched the blazer for a sexy black lace corset top, one that cinched her torso deliciously. Dominic couldn't keep his eyes off of her as Nina reached over to the side table, grabbing a glass of bubbly she had poured earlier.

"I just didn't want to aggravate the situation, which is why, I sort of… you know, put up with it! Trust me, I know it was wrong, but Jamie seemed really embarrassed and sympathetic towards me, so I kept up my job. Really pathetic, you probably think, right?" She circled the top of the glass, flashing puppy-dog eyes at Dominic, who was all ears. "Pathetic? Not even close. What you did is professional, no matter how you flip it. Unfortunately, you came all the way here to be a photographer for a wedding that included two dysfunctional people. How would you have known how bad it was going to be? There's no way! You did the best you could, and I think Jamie appreciates you for it. Because you know what, she's right. No other photographer would have taken that kind of treatment, especially from a groom-to-be. Ridiculous. I need another shot." Nina giggled as Dominic popped open the whiskey bottle and drank from its mouth. "Whoa there, cowboy. Slow down!" Dominic flashed crazy eyes, licking his lips as he gazed at the gorgeous photographer. He inched closer, sealing the gap between them. "I like when you call me a cowboy. Of course, *lawyer* would suffice, but cowboy just excites me more." Dominic rested the bottle of whiskey on the coffee table and placed a firm hand on Nina's thigh, causing her to look up at him teasingly. "What are you doing, Dominic? Are you trying to seduce me?" He placed his hand on his chest, as though to gesture that he was insulted.

"Trying, Nina? Touché. I don't have to try."

He leaned into her neck, planting warm kisses along the nape. "Dominic, please…"

"Shh, let me do my work. I know how to turn up outside of the courtroom, too." Nina laughed out loud, placing her hand on top of his head; her palm nearly disappeared in the bed of thick hair. "I don't know if I've told you this yet, but your hair is absolutely incredible." She hiccupped, covering her mouth bashfully.

"Are you drunk, Nina? Did I get you wasted?"

"Oh shut up, Dominic, I'm a light drinker."

"Let's get this glass out of your hands then, before you hurt yourself."

"No Dominic, let me finish my drink."

"Okay, okay! I won't push it."

Nina emptied her glass, keeping her eyes on Dominic the entire time. After a disastrous day, she was ready to let loose for a while. Resting the glass on the table, she let her ponytail down and tousled her hair, smoothing down the front and sides. "It's getting warm in here. Let's open up the balcony door or something, huh?" With a hop in his step, Dominic pushed open the door, allowing for a gusty wind to flow through the adorned suite. Nina flipped on the tv, browsing through channels as her thick hair rippled in the breeze. "Nothing good on tv these days, huh?" Dominic rejoined her on the sofa, resting his arm around her neck. "That's why I don't bother with cable. Just a waste, huh?" Dominic looked dashing in a button-down navy dress shirt and matching slacks.

Her inhibitions flying away with the breeze, Nina placed her hand on Dominic's leg, eyes still focused on the tv. "So, how was your time while I was gone? Meet any interesting characters?" Dominic groaned, thrashing his hair about. "Yeah, a group of ladies was acting a bit rowdy around the lunch hour. One of them was eyeing me pretty hard, but I tried burying my eyes in my paper to dodge the glares. To be honest, I thought they were your clients' guests at first. But damn, they were being so loud, they made it obvious that they were here to live it up and forget their cheating husbands."

Nina cocked her head back in laughter, glancing at Dominic in disbelief. "Forget their cheating husbands? They did not say that!"

"I couldn't believe it, either. It was so bizarre."

"Hey, you should have offered your legal services. I'm sure they would have been appreciative." Dominic roared in laughter, tapping her knee affectionately. "You're right, I should of. But then, they may have taken that as an invitation to sit down with me and get more information, and that just wasn't my scene." Nina rolled her eyes, continuing to flip through channels. "You sure that you wouldn't have liked that? A handsome man like you at a table full of beautiful women? How could you resist?"

"Beautiful women? Hardly. The only woman I have eyes for is you, believe you me."

"Oh yeah? And why me? Why a woman you've only just met? Why all of this, huh, Dominic? It's crazy if you think about it. You meet me on a plane, by chance, in my weakest state. Scared out of my mind; pathetic and terrified to sit my ass on a jet. And then, that's not even the kicker. Somehow, you turn out to be this handsome knight in shining armor, ready to hold my hand and escort me to the toilet. Like, who does that? Why me?"

Dominic stood up, holding his hands out for Nina to follow. Her incredible collarbone took center stage as she joined him under the brilliant glow of the room's chandelier, looking up at him nervously.

"There's no other right answer. You know, this sounds bizarre, and you're probably not going to believe me. But, believe it. I'm deep into horoscopes and things like that, okay? Yeah, save the laughs. A man who's supposed to be poised and stand on principles of fact, delving into talks about zodiac signs and all that they encompass? But I'm telling you, about two months ago, I got the strangest reading, and I feel like now, it all makes sense."

Nina wrinkled her nose, curious.

"A strange reading? Well, what did it say? Now, I really need to know."

Dominic bit back, unsure of how to continue.

"You sure you're not going to laugh?"

Nina's mouth hung open sarcastically as she crossed her arms over her chest.

"What, a confident, go-getter attorney like you, worried about a lady laughing at you? Hit me."

Dominic scoffed, but he played right into her hand.

"Yeah, well, okay. It's like they crafted the horoscope just for me. It said, 'The one you seek will be like none other. Look to the sky for answers.'"

Nina raised her hand in the air, heading to the side table for another drink.

"Really, Dominic? Did it really say that? You sure?"

He put his hands up in protest. "Why would I lie? Nina, don't you see? It makes so much sense. 'The one you seek will be like none other. Look to the sky for answers?' Are you kidding me? And look where I found you, thousands of feet above the clouds, at the right place and the right time. I'm telling you, it's fate. That's why I can't keep my eyes off of you, or keep my hands off of you. You're what I've been longing for. Yeah, lawyers like me have feelings. I've been hearing the disappointment in my parents' voices every time they ask me if I found a woman to make my wife. They had me when they were already in their 40s, you know? So, they've been longing for something like this to happen to me. I've damn near been manifesting you for most of my life, and here you are!"

Nina, shakily, eased herself onto the edge of the bed, Dominic's words hitting her hard. She gripped the edges, the tantalizing champagne doing its magic below the surface.

"Dominic, I don't know what to…" He rushed to her side and sat, swiftly placing his palm against her face. She sharply looked to the ground, the alcohol making her brain feel fuzzy and her body warm.

"I want you, Nina, I need you. Listen, we have a week here, so let's make the most of it. In my heart of hearts, I don't show people this side of me! In my heart of hearts, I know that everything happening right now is happening for a reason. What, are we supposed to just leave after this vacation, and never speak to each other again? Do you feel the energy between us, or am I just crazy?"

Nina bit her lip and turned to face him; her sultry eyes full of lust. "Of course, you're not crazy. The way we met is so unbelievable, and I'd be lying if I said I didn't feel something for you. In my worst moment, you were here at the ready to save the day. I came on this trip for two reasons. One, to face my fear of flying, and two, to support this client who simply wanted to get married overseas. Plus, I would get a vacation out of it! Little did I think I would have met you in the process, so no! I don't think you're crazy. You're a brilliant, intelligent, strong-willed man, and the past few days with you have shown me a lot about your character. You stand up for me, someone who you hardly know, and you're ready to defend whoever is in need. These are the qualities I always wished for in a man because I never saw these attributes in myself. You've given me more confidence in the past few days than childhood friends have given me in the last couple of years! And I mean that!"

"Just kiss me, already. A lawyer's time is precious." Dominic said hotly, flashing a toothy grin before locking lips with Nina, who was ready to receive everything Dominic had to offer.

"I know you wanted to take things slow, Nina. But please, understand, I can't do that. Don't hate me for

it, see me for what I am. I'm hungry for you, and I
want you to come back home with me, okay?"

He attacked her neck with kisses as he unhooked her
corset top, reveling in her moans as he did so.

"Dominic… mmm… Dom, don't stop." She
mumbled hurriedly; her throat thick with passion.

"You sure? You really mean that?" he sighed on her
neck, cupping her bosoms softly.

They met each other's lips and made out on the bed;
their hands exploring each other's bodies. The usually
well-composed lawyer was losing control with the
beautiful photographer thrashing in his arms.
Everything he could have dreamed of was right in
front of him at that very moment. Years of working
alongside gorgeous attorneys couldn't override what
he felt in that instance.

"You know, Nina," he started huskily, regretfully
pulling away from her.

"I've been thinking that maybe, just maybe, you
come with me to Wyoming. I know it's just nuts,
right? But hear me out. There's no way in hell that
I'm letting you go on that plane alone. And besides,
you need me! I know now how debilitating your
phobia is, and I want to be there for you every step of
the way. The thought of me leaving with you is
making me lose my composure, and believe me, this
is not a regular occurrence! The lawyer in me is
trying to make the right decision, the right call. This
is not one of the many cases that land on my desk on

a Monday morning. This is life." He clasped her hands in his, kissing them incessantly. Nina blushed, biting her lip as she stared at Dominic dreamily.

"Dom," she said weakly, but Dominic put a pause to her words as he locked lips with her, reveling in her taste and the scent of her floral perfume.

"I could never bore of you calling out my name. Please come with me. Leave whatever you had going on and stay with me in Wyoming. I have a few properties that I rent out, but the place I want you to be is in my main house, where I thrive and feel the best about myself. I want you to share my home with me so that I can take care of you."

Straightening up, though her mind still felt hazy from the bubbly, Nina stood up and began pacing the room, playing with her fingernails as she spoke.

"Move with you to Wyoming? Okay, Dominic, you've been more than accommodating to me. You know, you held my hand on the plane, helped me get through something I thought I'd never do again. Took a wad out of your wallet, gave it to me without hesitation. You're giving, there's no doubt. But move with you to another state? What would my parents think?" Dominic approached her surreptitiously, putting his hands on her waist. "How old are you, Nina?"

She looked down, taking a large gulp. "38."

"38! If you're 38 years old, why do you care about what your parents think? I know they raised you and all of that. We are on the same boat here. I had very supportive parents growing up, and I love them because they shaped me into the man I am today, but eventually, I left the nest, and even left the state! They're up in New Jersey as we speak. Of course, it was hard when I left; ma cried for a long time, and there were moments when I felt I was causing them more grief than anything else. However, I wanted to live a different life; Jersey was *not* it for me!" He rubbed her back affectionately as Nina held on to his every word.

"Nina, I will make sure every opportunity for you to grow your photography business will be yours to explore. My home is pretty much surrounded by nature and wildlife, something that would give you a perfect backdrop for your photography. Nina… please. I know it seems like I'm asking for too much; in fact, I would have to agree. To be frank, I'm falling for you, and I don't want to leave you behind after this vacation is over! Nina, I would fly my parents out to Wyoming to meet you personally, and I don't do that at all! Flying someone out to my home? If they wanted to see me, they'd find their own way, right? But no, this situation is not ordinary. I want my mom and dad to *know* you, and to see the brilliant woman that you are. Please, Nina. Will you come back to Wyoming with me?"

Nina couldn't believe what she was hearing, and it was almost too much to take. Without saying a word, she traversed to the balcony door and opened it, stepping onto the platform. She welcomed the cool nightly breeze as it enveloped her. Dominic's dress shoes clacked against the ground as he approached her from behind and pulled her close to him, staring off into the calm waters of the sea below them.

"I love Turks and Caicos. So serene."

Dominic kissed her neck, refusing to let go of Nina this time. He spun her around to face him and gave her a final kiss before donning pleading eyes.

Nina gave a deep sigh, biting the skin around her fingernails. "Dominic, everything I have is in Illinois! All my belongings, my parents, everything!"

Dominic smirked, looking down at Nina's manicured nails and toying with them for a moment. Then, without missing a beat, he pulled a ring box out of his trouser pocket and opened it, revealing a stunningly ornate silver ring with a turquoise gem. Nina gasped as Dominic slid the stunning ring onto her finger. She slowly raised her hand in front of her face. The moonlight illuminated her new piece of jewelry.

"Dominic, what? How? Why?"

Dominic laughed but got very intense, staring at Nina in her eyes. "While you were gone, I went into town and met with a jeweler. I wanted to get a ring with the colors you were wearing when I saw you on the plane. This is a promise ring; a sign of the devotion that I have towards you. I need you."

Dashed Dreams

"My mom couldn't believe what I told her. Me, moving to Wyoming with a man I found on a plane? Thank god she has my dad; with his expertise, he could have resuscitated her if necessary." Nina commented freely, as Dominic nearly fell over in a fit of laughter. The pair were collecting their belongings after enjoying all Turks & Caicos had to offer.

Parasailing, swimming, running along the beach. It was a fun-filled, warm, and tropical experience that neither was eager to soon forget. The night before, they attended a salsa dance that took place in Onyx's lobby, and many couples enjoyed swaying to the upbeat, melodic tunes. Nina, being shy, initially refused to stand up and join the crowd. "I swear, Dominic, I have two left feet. I'll save you the embarrassment." Dominic rolled his eyes, holding his hands out and refusing to take no for an answer.

Hesitantly, she got up and Dominic swiftly pulled her body close to his, flashing a delicious smile as his eyes remained locked on Nina. She looked dazzling in a spaghetti-strap, navy blue maxi dress with silver sequins lining the bodice. Other vacationers murmured as they watched Nina and Dominic soaking up the night, swaying with the music as though no one in the room mattered.

"See, it's easy! Just follow my lead."

Nina, overcome with giggles, stayed quiet and indeed followed the lawyer's movements, mimicking him in cadence. At some point, she cocked her head back in laughter, taking stock of the people around them who had moved farther back, essentially creating a circle around the pair. "Dominic, they're all watching us." Dominic confidently glanced around the lobby, taking in the scene before bringing his focus back to Nina.

"I don't blame them. We're a sight to behold. This was all meant to be." He twirled Nina sensually, the ends of her dress fluttering lightly against the glistening marble floor. Dominic ravished her with his eyes as they traversed the floor smoothly, not missing a beat. It was a night they'd never forget.

"Yeah, I suppose him being a cardiologist comes in handy! But honestly, what does she think about you literally uprooting everything, and moving to another state? Does she think you're crazy?"

Nina folded her clothing at lightning speed, looking up at Dom as she did so. "It's so weird, you know? My parents are very logical people, and it's understandable if you see their line of work, and what's expected of them. But oddly enough, they both took it very well. I mean, they already think of this as a prodigious feat on my end. I literally had severe PTSD from that experience when I was a teen. No one around me thought I would get over it. I guess after explaining our divine encounter, they believe all of this to be a great thing for me! Honestly, they're saying they want to meet you and know who this lawyer is!" Dominic brushed his hair back dramatically. "I can't wait to see them. So, movers, how soon should I get that arranged?" Nina thought for a moment as she glanced up at the sexy lawyer, who seemed to always look great, no matter what he was wearing or doing.

"Let's do it asap. The sooner, the better, right?"

Dominic gave her an air-five as he placed the last items in his suitcase and looked around the room, contented they had kept it in a suitable condition.

"We did pretty well, you and I, huh? It's like we were never here!" Nina rolled her eyes as she adjusted the collar of her shirt. "Yeah, because we were hardly in here. We spent most of our time outdoors, right?"

"Yeah, you're right. Damn, you really make logic so simple. It's one of those things about being a lawyer kind of unfortunate. You have to drive home your facts and make profound stances to prove your point, when sometimes the answers are quite simple and easy to get to. I need to work on that."

Nina walked over to him and placed her hands on his chest, tracing her fingers along with his defined abs.

"Well, you helped me a lot, and I know now that you want to continue to do so, so let me help you, Mr. Lawyer. Maybe I can be your assistant?" Dominic's eyes expanded with desire as he laid kisses on her cheeks and nibbled on her ear lightly, enjoying her writhing in his grasp. "I think I'd like that."

After checkout, the duo packed up their suitcases and bid farewell to their home for a week, truly regretful that their vacation came to a close so rapidly. Piling into the vehicle and traversing down the road for the last time, the Onyx faded into the background. Nina rubbed her hands together anxiously in the passenger seat, observing the palm trees' leaves dancing in the breeze. "You know Dominic, that feeling is coming back. You know, heading back to the airport, boarding the plane. This has all been wonderful, but we can't forget what drew us together in the first place; my phobia of flying on planes. It's been such an amazing experience, I managed to push my feelings of trepidation and worry out of my mind, but now, they're coming back." Dominic lulled Nina softly, rubbing her bare thigh with his hand as he maneuvered the wheel with the other.

"Nina, we've been over this so many times. You're safe and sound with me. The way we met was divine, as you said in your own words. I can think of a thousand different ways to describe what I felt when I first laid eyes on you, but I'm working on my redundancy, you know?" Nina giggled as Dominic bit his lower lip, lightly tapping her leg with his open palm.

"I'm just eager to get on the plane, get to Illinois, meet your parents, pack everything up, scoop you and take you to my oasis. This has been the highlight of my life! Meeting you changed everything. Whenever you get doubtful, look at the ring I placed on your finger. It's more symbolic than you think!" Nina obediently glanced at her hand, admiring the remarkable ring. Dominic was right. He had been right the entire time, and Nina, still processing everything that had transpired between them, was ready to start anew and move forward with Dominic in her corner. "I know you're right, Dominic. You'll have to deal with all of this, you know! The nervousness and anxiety… I can get difficult, I don't want to hold you back." Dominic scoffed, speeding slightly to pass a slow-moving vehicle. "Difficult? There's not a damn thing in this world I'd leave you for. I've seen difficult, believe me, and you come nowhere close to that. I'll be here every step of the way of your journey. In fact, your journey is mine, too. I want to go where you go. I love everything about you because that's what makes you unique. Remember that."

The rest of the car ride was hushed, and soon after, they arrived at the airport. Dominic processed for the rental car for return as Nina sat on a chair, glancing around the airport nervously.

Dominic wants me to stay calm. I know he does, but he doesn't fully understand how triggering this place is to me, she thought to herself as every sound in the space was setting her off. A boy on a skateboard whizzed past her, the sudden rush of air hitting her face like a ton of bricks. She sat back, startled, with her palm delicately running across her chest. Dominic was making his way towards her, holding a handful of documents, and wearing an affectionate smile. It quickly receded as he saw Nina's panicked expression. Sitting beside her, he rubbed her back, attempting to pacify her. "I'm here, Nina. It's okay, everything's going to be fine."

"Flight 545 to Chicago, Illinois. Please head to gate 3 for boarding." An announcement rang out over the intercom, jolting Nina in her seat. Dominic pressed his lips together, summoning Nina to stand. "That's us, Nina. Everything's just fine, okay? I'm here. Let's head on the plane! We'll do the same thing we did when we met a week ago, alright? I'll hold your hand, take you to the washroom, anything you want, okay? Wouldn't want you to have any accidents, huh?" He lovingly toyed with her chin.

Apprehensively, Nina joined hands with Dominic and made her way to Gate 3, where there were two attendants, a man, and a woman, ushering people through the open door leading to the airplane. As they walked, Nina felt the sensation that the path she was traversing was becoming elongated as she inched closer to the gate door. She halted for a moment, rubbing her temples as Dominic held onto her, concern etched across his eyebrows.

"Hey, Nina! Hey, listen, I'm here, baby."

Nina slowly looked up at him just as his gaze fell to the floor. His chin quivered with anticipation. "Baby?" she repeated, the sensation of butterflies in her stomach rampant.

"Yeah, I said what I said, and what about it?" Clinging onto his hand, Nina kept her head up and marched to the gate, keeping her gaze pinpointed on the long corridor before her.

The male attendant checked their tickets and gave them a friendly nod, gesturing to the hallway.

"Enjoy your flight, guys!" Dominic nodded appreciatively at the man as he clasped Nina's hand and led her down the path until they reached the entrance of the plane. Nina looked down at their tickets timidly. "Looks like we're in the front this time; that definitely eases my worries." She said dryly, shuffling to the location. Dominic massaged her neck, dodging people that were in the way. "Hey now, you've got to see the beauty in everything, Nina! We'll be one of the first to come off the plane when we land. That's gotta be a plus!" Nina shrugged her shoulders, considering his point.

"Yeah, I guess that's true. I think I'll be needing a shot after this is all said and done." Dominic raised a hand in agreement. "Anything you want, I'll get it for you. Once we get to cruising altitude, if you want the entire menu, it's yours. I won't let you have a bad time on this flight, or any flight, for that matter." Finding their seats, Nina flashed him a quizzical look.

"Any flight? What, you plan on taking me on trips around the world?" Dominic moved slowly towards the window seat, promptly closing the window out of consideration for Nina.

"Any man would be crazy to *not* take you around the world. A woman like you deserves to be treated like a queen. When we arrive in Wyoming, though, you may not even feel like traveling again. The state, on its own, is so breathtaking that it isn't really that surprising to think about why this trip to Turks and Caicos was a unique excursion for me. Damn, my backyard is essentially a retreat. You'll see what I mean when we get there."

 He squeezed her hand as Nina watched the masses of people traversing to their seats. Plenty of children were on the flight, far more than there were on flight 565. After a while, a handsome but short male flight attendant began giving verbal instructions for in-flight safety, and Nina and Dominic closely watched, following along as they did the first time.

"This is your captain speaking! Welcome, everyone, to flight 545 from Turks and Caicos to Chicago, Illinois. The weather is calling for some gust winds, so we may hit a pocket of turbulence once we're in the air. Please keep that in mind. Entertainment is right at your fingertips; please enjoy in-flight movies and shows, and thank you kindly for choosing Palumbo Airlines today. Enjoy the flight."

Nina's heart was thudding in her chest as she reached for Dominic's hand. "See, turbulence again, Dom! Why does this even exist?" Dominic burst out laughing, his eyes smiling as he looked at a very anxious Nina, who was writhing with discomfort. "Turbulence is agitating; there's no doubt about it, but they expertly trained these guys in the cockpit for situations like this. It's like a doctor diagnosing someone with the flu. It's second nature to them; they know how to navigate it and combat the situation so that things stay on course." He leaned in and softly kissed her on the lips, subduing her with his overwhelming, intoxicating love. "Just hold me, and don't let go, okay?" Nina drew in a breath and held it momentarily before exhaling. A kind-faced flight attendant approached their seats, clearly noticing Nina's distress. "Everything okay, ma'am? We're about to take off." Nina nodded quickly, trying to catch her breath. The flight attendant glanced at Dominic, concerned for Nina's well-being. "Okay, no problem. Please be sure to fasten your seatbelts. Before long, we'll be in the air." She gave a cheery smile and made her way to her seat, joining her colleagues. The plane began rolling to its takeoff position, and Nina shifted uneasily, anxiously peering around the cabin of the jet. It began picking up speed as it taxied down the runway. As the nose of the plane rose off the tarmac, Nina pushed her head back and squeezed Dominic's hand, gesturing to her mouth.

"Gum," she mouthed, but she couldn't speak, because no words came out. Nodding sympathetically, he took a stick out of his pocket and popped it in her mouth, clasping onto her hand as their heads rocked back and forth against their headrests. The entire cabin rocked violently and for a brief moment, Nina looked at Dominic, who was gritting his teeth through the discomfort. Sensing her eyes were on him, he looked at her with eyes that seemed to have their own light source. As his head tumbled from side to side, he managed to lean forward and kiss her, never letting go of her hand. "Wyoming, Wyoming," he croaked out. A sudden flash of light blinded them, and abruptly, Nina got up from her cushioned seat, unable to take anymore. She rubbed her arms in a pacifying fashion.

"No, I refuse to believe this happened! Please tell me this isn't true." Dominic stood next to her, dressed in a brilliant ivory robe. He rested his hands on her shoulders, which felt as soft as silk. Nina wore a champagne-toned, billowy gown that had an extensive train trailing far behind her. Her hair hung

loosely past her shoulders; elegant curls that moved
graciously with every movement. She was immersed
in the clouds; the breeze rippling between her and
Dominic, who wouldn't take his eyes off of her.

"Dominic, what did I just watch? Are you trying to
say that everything we did was my imagination?
Dom, LISTEN! We went to Turks and Caicos, right?
The restaurants, the wedding, come on, work with
me, Dominic, you gave me a ring." She looked down
at her hand, but it was void of any jewelry. Her throat
tightened as a strident voice echoed through the
vastness of the sky, causing Nina to cover her ears in
fear. Dominic stroked her cheeks, lulling her.

"Nina, you did not make it to Turks and Caicos,
because you perished on Salvo Airlines flight 965.
There were no survivors."